Corbenic

Corbenic

CATHERINE FISHER

Greenwillow Books
An Imprint of HarperCollins *Publishers*

Acknowledgments

Epigraphs by kind permission of the translators: Nigel Bryant, "Conte du Graal,"
from *Perceval: The Story of the Grail,* by Chretien de Troyes (D. S. Brewer, 1982);
John Matthews, "Oianau of Merlin," from *Merlin through the Ages* (Blandford, 1995);
T. Jones and G. Jones, "Peredur Son of Efrawg" from *The Mabinogion*
(Everyman Classics, 1949).

Corbenic
Copyright © 2002 by Catherine Fisher
First published in 2002 in Great Britain by Red Fox Books,
an imprint of Random House Children's Books.
First published in 2006 in the United States by Greenwillow Books.

The right of Catherine Fisher to be identified as the author
of this work has been asserted by her.

The text of this book is set in AGaramond.
Book design by Sylvie Le Floc'h.

Library of Congress Cataloging-in-Publication Data
Fisher, Catherine
Corbenic / by Catherine Fisher.
p. cm.
"Greenwillow Books."
Summary: In this modern-day version of Perceval and the Holy Grail,
a guilt-ridden British teenager leaves his mentally ill mother to live with his wealthy
uncle and begins a journey of self-knowledge and redemption after being briefly
transported to the Waste Land of Arthurian times.
ISBN-10: 0-06-072470-6 (trade bdg.) ISBN-13: 978-0-06-072470-2
ISBN-10: 0-06-072471-4 (lib. bdg.) ISBN-13: 978-0-06-072471-9
[1. Mothers and sons—Fiction. 2. Grail—Fiction. 3. Identity—Fiction.
4. Space and time—Fiction. 5. Coming of age—Fiction. 6. England—Fiction.]
PZ7.F4995Co 2006 [Fic]—dc22 2003056866

First American Edition 10 9 8 7 6 5 4 3 2 1

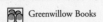 Greenwillow Books

✠ Sword ✠

✶ One ✶

His mother kept him there and held him back...

Conte du Graal

Very far away, the voice said, "Who drinks from the Grail?"

Jerked out of a doze, Cal opened his eyes. Then he tugged the earphones off and rubbed his face wearily. The woman who had been sitting next to him must have gotten off at the last station; now her seat was empty. A man in uniform was wheeling a trolley down the aisle of the train; it was crammed with crisps and sandwiches and piles of upturned plastic cups around the shiny urn. The man caught Cal's eye. "Drinks? Tea? Coffee?"

It would be embarrassing to say no, so he muttered, "Tea," knowing it would be the cheapest thing. Then he dragged some coins out of his pocket and sorted through them, trying to look careless, as if money didn't matter.

The train was a lot emptier now. It rattled viciously over some points; the trolley man swayed, balancing expertly in the aisle as he filled a plastic cup under the tap, the trolley rocking so that a small packet of biscuits slid off onto the empty seat. Chocolate digestives. Cal scowled. He was so hungry he almost felt sick. "Those too."

Outside, wet fields flashed by, and some houses in a scatter of dead leaves. The man leaned over and flipped down the small table at the back of the seat, clipped the lid on the tea and put it down. A tiny bag of sugar. Milk. A plastic stirrer. The train clattered; Cal grabbed the hot cup in alarm.

"One pound thirty, sir, thank you."

Sir. For a moment he thought the joker was making fun of him and glared up, but the man's face was closed and polite, and once he had the money he trundled away up the carriage resuming his smooth, "Tea? Drinks?"

Cal leaned back and looked at the plastic cup with distaste. He hated tea. Coffee was more upmarket. He unclipped the lid and stirred the tea bag gloomily. When he'd made some money he'd really spend; travel first class where they had white china and linen, everything of the best. They'd call him sir and mean it then. He peeled the metal top from the milk and it sprayed everywhere. He swore aloud. The woman opposite glared at him. He glared back, scrubbing his jacket. This had cost. It wasn't designer but it looked it. Or he hoped it did. The momentary fear that it looked cheap slid under his guard, but he squashed it hastily. Pulling the earphones back on, he let the music blast out the train noise, dipping a biscuit in the tea and watching the landscape through his own reflection.

He'd been on this train all day. It had left Bangor at nine that morning, late, so that his mother had lingered on the platform, tearful, her hasty makeup a mess, telling him to phone, going on and on about how much she'd miss him, couldn't manage without him, about coming back for weekends, about keeping his room the same. His room! He thought of the little box with its grubby paper and the neighbor's baby wailing through the walls. He was well shot of that.

Uncomfortable, he shifted. Why had she had to come? Anyone might have seen her, and as usual she'd been barely sober from the night before. He'd gone to find a seat long before the train started; still she had tapped on the glass and waved and cried at the window. Remembering her crumpled misery and runny mascara, his hand clenched on the empty cup; he felt the plastic crackle and then crushed it slowly. His face was hot. But the weak tea had made him feel better, and the biscuits. He hadn't eaten anything since breakfast, and he'd gotten that himself, as he always did.

The train slid into a station, brakes screeching. Cal rubbed a circle of damp off the glass and looked out. Craven Arms, the sign read. Another place he'd never heard of. Mountains, a few people running under umbrellas, the bare platform plastered with clotting autumn leaves. Like all the rest of the stations that day.

As they pulled out, the carriage lights went on. All at once, outside it seemed dark, the early dusk of November. Hills closed in as the train ran below them; odd craggy ridges, tree-covered. Most people had gotten off; no one had gotten on. Once, a mobile phone burbled stupid music; far down at the end the refreshments bloke was reading a paper with his feet on the opposite seat.

Cal leaned back, yawning. He was so tired of sitting still, so stiff. The music was tinny, the batteries fading; he flicked it off with a groan and immediately the rhythmic clatter of the train came back, rocking him, comforting. He had at least another hour till Chepstow. Through the steamy windows he could only see himself, looking crumpled, and then very faintly a line of high forestry dark against the twilight. In a farmhouse the windows were lit, looking warm and snug. A girl walking a dog waved to the speeding train. He wrapped his coat around him, and closed his eyes. As the train roared into the blackness of the tunnel, he put his feet up on the seat, leaning awkwardly with his head against the window. It would be all right now. He'd planned this for years; he'd made the break. Life would be different. His uncle would meet him in some big, flashy car. He wouldn't have to see her anymore. He wouldn't have to hide the knives and the bottles ever again.

✤ ✤ ✤

6

He woke abruptly. A voice was crackling over the PA. Somewhere in his head the echo of what it had said was just out of reach, but it had been Chepstow, he was suddenly, coldly sure. The train was already stopping; outside, a lamp loomed close to the window.

Cal panicked. The train was empty. He scrambled up, confused. Dregs of tea from the crumpled cup spilled on him; he grabbed his coat, jerked his rucksack down from the rack and ran, past tea-stained tables and abandoned newspapers. Outside the windows it was pitch dark. He jabbed the door button anxiously; as the doors swooshed open he jumped out and looked up the length of the train.

"Hey! Excuse me!"

Far down in the frosty dark the guard stepped back into the train. Doors slid shut. Cal yelled, "Wait! Listen! I need to know if this is . . ."

His voice was lost in the roar of the engine; the train was moving, gaining speed, and he ran after it, and saw through the flashing windows the dripping sign in the hedge opposite. It said:

CORBENIC

"Bloody *hell*!" he hissed furiously.

But the train was a rattle in the dimness, one red light. Tree shadows closed over it. And then it had gone.

The night was suddenly, utterly silent. So silent he could

hear every drip from the trees. He flung the rucksack down in fury and looked around, unable to believe he'd been so stupid, so absolutely stupid! Where the hell was this? Why had he thought it was his stop? Raging at himself he shrugged his jacket on, shivering uncontrollably after the warmth of the train. The platform was deserted, gleaming with rain, lit by one dim lamp, the pool of light from it glinting with drips. God, this was the middle of nowhere! Looking around he saw only the dark clustering shapes of trees; above them a bank of cloud loomed, torn by the wind to show fleeting, frosty stars.

There had to be someone, a ticket office. He turned. "Hello. Anyone here?" His voice rang, echoing. Wind whipped leaves in his face. There was no station building, no waiting room, nothing but the small wet platform, the dripping lamp, a fence with a creaking gate. And silence.

His breath smoked in the damp air. He shook his head, bleakly. This was a disaster. But there would be a timetable. Outside, by the fence.

Dragging up the heavy rucksack he tugged it on, the weight making him groan. Then he crossed the wet platform to the gate in the hedge. It hung awkwardly on its hinges, and creaked in the wind. The white paint was blistered and old. He leaned over, getting soaked, his hands frozen, and found there was no timetable, nothing at all but the gate, and a dim lane that ran into utter darkness in both directions.

Cal swore in dismay. He stood under the dripping trees

and knew that all around him the night was empty. For a moment the old panic threatened him; then he shoved his hands in his pockets and took a cold breath. Get a grip. Get the next train, that was all. Just get the next train. But when would it come? Would it even stop at this godforsaken hole? He crushed the despair as he'd taught himself to do, over and over. It would be okay. He'd have to wait.

There was nowhere to sit. The bare platform ran with puddles. He leaned against the lamp and the rain pattered around him, the great trees overhead sighing and swishing every time the wind moved them, sending a cascade of icy drops to soak his shoulders and splash his shoes. His clean shoes. He looked at his watch. The tiny green numbers said 5:40.

Ten minutes later he had dumped the rucksack and was walking up and down, the tap of his footsteps loud in the hush. At least he thought it was ten minutes, but when he looked at the watch again it told exactly the same time, 5:40, and he couldn't believe this. The watch had stopped, maybe hours ago. He kicked the lamp in fury, and as if in some sort of revenge, the rain immediately came down harder, drumming steadily through the leaves, a thrumming downpour.

He couldn't stand it anymore. Doubts had begun to creep in; he couldn't keep them out. What if there was no train; what if he had to stay here all night? His uncle would go to the station and not find him, and he'd ring Bangor and his mother . . . Cal closed his eyes in despair, then opened them.

A phone! All he needed was a stupid phone. There had to be one near. If he'd had a mobile . . . if he'd bought one instead of this useless jacket that was letting the rain in . . . But he hadn't. So he'd have to go and find one.

It was hard to leave the platform; he dithered, waiting, sure that as soon as he turned his back a train would come, but at last he was so stiff and soaked and fed up that he hauled up his rucksack and splashed back to the gate. The wood was swollen; it took both hands to force open, as if no one had used it for years. He squeezed through, shoved his wet fingers in his pockets, and looked up and down the lane. Dark trees met overhead.

He turned right, walking quickly, trying to get warm. His breath clouded the damp air, his footsteps crunching unnaturally loudly on the muddy, puddled track; all around him the night cascaded and pattered and dripped with falling water. Scowling, he dragged his collar up. Someone must live here. Somewhere.

The lane was lonely. Scary. It became a gloomy tunnel, a swishing, pine-smelling dimness, and as he trudged the mud was slippery with great drifts of soaked leaves. Small noises disturbed him: the snap of a twig, rustles, and soft fallings. He walked faster, trying not to imagine being followed, dark shapes jumping out from the trees, but he was rushing, he couldn't help it and the panic was back. After what he thought was about half a mile he stopped, heart thudding, an ache in his side so sharp he could barely catch his breath. He knew he was scared. Anyone might be down here. Murderers. Nutcases. He should go back. He might be walking for hours.

A screech. It was tiny, and high, and it made him jump with terror before he told himself it was a mouse, a stupid mouse. An owl, or a mouse.

He wished he had a weapon. If he could find a thick stick . . .

Clutching his side he breathed in the damp air. His nose was running; he wiped it wearily on his ironed handkerchief and pushed the wet hair off his face, wishing hopelessly for the warm train, turning and looking back into the pitch-black lane. It would be worse going back. He'd come too far already.

Then he heard a splash. It was loud, as if something had plopped into water. Below him. To the right.

Cal breathed out slowly. The noise of the downpour was unbelievably loud, but this had been different. He took a step toward the trees. They were thickly massed. He looked down and saw a steep overgrown incline, dark with brambles and undergrowth, its rich smell of rot and soil rising to him. Down there was water, maybe a lake. It trickled and lapped; he saw glints of it in the dimness. And faintly, above the pattering rain, he was sure he could hear voices. Then, between the wet black trunks, brilliant as lightning, a flash-light flickered.

He straightened up, breathing hard, listening. Poachers? Gamekeepers, maybe. He didn't know and he didn't care. He was too wet to care, and the thought of the empty, terrifying lane that might go on for miles and miles filled him with despair. It was dangerous—they could be anyone. But he had to find a phone. He squeezed his hair back, feeling the rain from it run down his back. A great leaf plastered itself to his face and he snatched it away in hissed panic; maybe it was the fright that finally made him shout.

"Hey!" he yelled recklessly. "Hey, you down there. Hello! Can you hear me?"

The night poured on his shoulders. It seemed an age before someone said, "We hear you."

The flashlight came on again. He glimpsed a tiny boat, a flimsy wicker thing tethered to the bank, the long line slack in the water, and two dim figures looking up at him. The beam of light moved up the bank till it hit Cal's face, and he put his hand up against it crossly. "Cut it out!"

But the light stayed on him a long moment. Then it bounced off the trees till he saw one of the fishermen clearly; a bulky man, standing awkwardly. The other was slighter, dark-haired, sitting with a net over his knees.

"What are you looking for?" the big man called, his voice deep over the rain-patter.

"I'm lost. Is there a phone near here? Have you got one I could use?"

To Cal's surprise, the man laughed, a low, humorless sound. "Why?"

"So they can come and pick me up from home. I got off the train at the wrong station."

The dark-haired man, sitting down, said quietly, "Have you any idea where you are?"

Cal felt annoyed. Then he remembered the station sign. "Corbenic."

The man said something to his friend. The bigger one nodded, and looked up. "You must go on to the Castle."

"Castle?"

"Hotel. About a mile on."

The wind blew Cal's hair into his eyes. "Great," he muttered sourly. But he was immensely relieved.

There was a splash as if the fishermen had dropped the nets over the side. "There's nowhere else," the deep voice said. "This is the Waste Land. Nowhere else for miles."

Uneasy, Cal said, "Do they get many visitors?"

"Not so many as they used to." The flashlight flickered over Cal's face. "Tell them we sent you."

Rain spattered. "Thanks," Cal yelled. But as he turned away the other man, the dark one, said, "Wait!" He looked up; Cal saw even at this distance that he was pale, almost gaunt, his eyes dark hollows. "Are you sure you're ready?" he whispered, his voice anxious, deeply troubled.

"What?"

"You need to be ready. Or it will be a long journey for all of us."

Cal frowned. "I thought your mate said about a mile?"

The fisherman shook his head, almost sadly, and the flashlight went out. "So he did. So he did."

Uneasy, Cal climbed back up onto the track and trudged on. He felt worn out and it was hard to think. A hotel. Lucky. He might be miles from Chepstow. His uncle wouldn't come. And his mother would be down at Murphy's by this time anyway, and be past caring either way.

He was so wet now he didn't care about the jacket or the drenched boots; rain trickled into every crease of him, even his pockets, and his clothes felt heavy and sopping. He was almost running down the dark leafy tunnel of the lane.

And finally, around the bend, the hedge became a wall, a high red-brick wall smothered with glossy wet ivy, the trees behind it black and ominous. He squelched alongside it, seeing how the track was a mire of mud here, and at the muddiest place of all he found a wooden door, and above that a sign that swung and creaked and dripped on his face.

CASTLE HOTEL
CORBENIC

The letters were worn, and rain-streaked. Below them, cracked and badly painted, was the pub sign, but instead of a castle all it showed was a crooked yellow chalice. And hanging from that on rusty hooks, swinging so wildly he could barely make it out, a tiny addition read:

VACANCIES

✦ Two ✦

A sorry figure in a court so distinguished as that.

Peredur

There was nothing to knock, but his groping fingers found a latch under the dripping screen of ivy; he lifted it, and the door opened. Beyond the arch was a shadowy garden, blackened by frost. Bare branches dripped onto a gravel path. The trees were dead or leafless.

Cal stepped through, holding the door open. It didn't look promising, and it was too quiet. Maybe the place was closed up. Out of season. Maybe they were all in bed.

He let the door swing behind him with a soft clink. He'd find out. There was no way he was walking back up that lane.

The gravel crunched under his feet. On each side of the dim path small statues peered from among the withered plants: peculiarly crouched animals, bears and cats and tiny foxes whose eyes gleamed fleetingly in wet faces. He passed them quietly, choked with an odd feeling of excitement. The rich stink of the clotting leaves seeming sharper here, the watching animals tense, as if ready to pounce on his back. It made him remember a picture in a book he'd seen when he was small, of a garden of sleeping princes all tangled in thorns, and beyond them, high and gray and sinister, the walls of the castle, with one light in a high window. He had forgotten it till now. For a second, he remembered how the story had made him feel, the flavor of it.

There was a light here too. It flickered through the branches; he had to bend down and peer ahead to see it, because the trees were so tangled and low, and for a moment he thought it was a bundle of burning wooden sticks in a bracket on the wall. But pushing through the stiff branches he found that the trees grew right up to the stonework and at the path's end was a black wrought-iron lantern with a dim electric bulb inside.

Above him the house was a shadow. He couldn't even make out what it looked like, except that it was big, and old, and ivy covered the walls. Over the door a sort of mock portcullis jabbed its pointed spikes down at him. There was a porch, littered in the corner with heaps of windblown leaves and, at last, a bellpull with a heavy, faceted knob, swinging in the wind. Cal caught it in his numbed fingers; water dripped from it, cold as ice, the night silent around him. For a moment he stood there, undecided, afraid of the place, of who might be there.

Then he pulled the bell. It jangled deep inside the building. Lights came on; they flooded his face and he saw the panels of the door were stained glass, a rainbow patchwork of knights and horses, their heraldry bright with golds and blues and scarlet. Upstairs windows lit; he heard voices, the sound of some sort of horn or trumpet, the rattle and clatter of dishes. For a moment he almost felt he had wakened the place from a centuries-long sleep; then he noticed the stone at the end of the bellpull in his hand was as red and glittering as a ruby, and stared at it in amazement.

The door opened. Warmth came out and embraced him; for a second the relief of that was so great he couldn't speak. A woman stood there, tall and gray-haired, wearing a long dress of some rich velvet. "Welcome to the Castle," she said gently.

He had his speech all ready. "I'm sorry to bother you so late, but . . ."

The woman smiled and stepped back. "Please! You're soaked, and cold. Come inside. It's too evil a night to be on the road."

"I haven't . . . I mean I just need to use the phone. Do you have a phone?"

"Yes. We have everything you need. Come in."

He followed her over the threshold, into a hall panelled with dark wood. It was dazzlingly lit with expensive-looking marble lamps. A huge round table stood in the hall's center, with some sort of sword on a stand; on all the walls red brocade wallpaper glowed, and in a vast hearth between two suits of armor a log fire roared and crackled.

Classy, Cal thought. He eased the dripping rucksack off and dumped it on the floor. He felt cheap and wet and thoroughly out of place.

"While you call," the woman said kindly, "I'll have your room made ready."

A room! Cal stared, alarmed. "Oh no! I mean, I won't be staying. I'm just going to get someone to pick me up."

She shook her head. "From here? I doubt it."

"My uncle will. Well . . . how far are we from Chepstow?"

"As far from there as from anywhere, I'm afraid." The woman knelt and put another log on the fire carefully, the wide sleeves of her dress slipping back to show strong arms. She looked up at him. "This is the Waste Land. But the room won't be expensive, if that's what worries you. You're our guest, and there's no charge."

That really scared him. Nothing, absolutely nothing, ever came free. Whatever sort of weird setup he had wandered into here had to be dodgy. Phone, then get out, he thought.

As if she guessed the woman stood, wiping her fingers on a lace-edged handkerchief. "There's the phone." She nodded behind him. It was an old-fashioned sort of booth in the corner of the corridor.

Cal said, "Thanks," and headed for it quickly.

A door opened and closed somewhere in the building; he heard music and a rumor of voices, shut off, instantly.

The booth had no door and smelled of lavender. When he'd picked up the receiver and turned the woman had gone, so he dialed his uncle's number quickly. It was an ancient Bakelite machine, black and heavy with a silver dial that spun with a satisfying purr, the words CORBENIC 301000 printed in the center.

There was a crackle, the ringing tone. Then, oddly small and distant, his uncle's voice. "Hello?"

"Uncle Trevor? It's Cal."

"Cal? Where are you?" He didn't sound anxious. More surprised. "Is your train in early?"

"No. Look . . ." Cal took a deep breath, hating himself. "I made a mistake. I got off at the wrong stop."

He heard his uncle's hiss of annoyance. "How on earth did you manage that! Where are you?"

Cal ignored the first question. "Somewhere called Corbenic."

"Never heard of it."

"No. I think it's sort of out in the sticks. The last station I remember before it was Craven Arms, but . . ."

"*Craven Arms!* That's about three hours' drive!"

Cal scowled. He felt a total fool, and suddenly knew what was coming. When his uncle spoke again he sounded even more distant, as if he'd stepped back. He was also brisk and matter-of-fact. "It's far too far for me to pick you up. I'm going out later anyway. You'll have to stay over. Where are you ringing from?"

"A hotel. The Castle. But I . . ."

"Is it all right?"

"What do you mean?"

"For heaven's sake, Cal! Is it decent? How many stars has it got?"

He had no idea. Wearily he looked around at the paneled hall, the crackling fire. "It's posh. It'll cost an arm and a leg."

"Don't pay more than forty pounds for the night. Have you got that much on you? If not, get them to phone me in the morning and I'll settle it by credit card, but I warn you, Cal, I'm not making a habit of this."

"No," Cal said tightly. "Neither am I."

"Keep to yourself. Don't talk to strangers."

"I'm not a kid."

"Well then, be discreet. Don't make a fool of yourself. And for God's sake get the right train in the morning and call me from the station." He sighed, sourly. "I'll ring Annie."

"She'll be at the pub," Cal said, reluctantly.

"Yes. I know what state she'll be in too." His uncle's voice was rich with distaste. "To be honest I don't suppose it's worth bothering. She probably won't even remember you're gone." The phone went dead with an irritated click.

"And good night to you too." Cal dropped the receiver

21

and stared blankly at the paneled wall. Out of nowhere, lone-liness flooded him like a wave. For a moment he knew with devastating clarity that no one in his family knew where he was or even cared that much. Trevor didn't want him. It went through him like a coldness. Like shock.

"Your mother will be concerned."

He turned quickly. The man watching him was sitting in a chair; that was Cal's first thought. Then he realized it was a wheelchair. The man was watching him closely. "Won't she?"

"No." Cal came out of the booth. "She's not bothered."

"I see. But you found my castle. I told you it wasn't far."

The fisherman. The dark man in the boat. It was him. Close up he was younger; his hair a little too long, his knees covered in a warm tartan rug. But his face was still drawn, as if some secret pain consumed him.

"Your castle?" Cal said quietly.

The man's smile was brief. "I should have said so but it wasn't a ploy for custom, I assure you. There really is nowhere else for you to go." He held out a frail hand. "My name is Alain Bron."

Cal shook hands awkwardly. "Cal. Well, everyone calls me Cal. Look, I'm sorry, but I am going to have to stay here tonight."

The dark-haired man nodded gravely. "Of course you are. Everyone always does." His green eyes watched Cal so intently Cal felt hotly self-conscious. The old worries came flooding up; his clothes, his accent. He must look cheap. As if he couldn't pay.

But Bron only said, almost to himself, "You are the one, aren't you." He was trembling.

A door opened behind them. A man wearing a peculiar, almost medieval robe trimmed with fur came out and crossed the hall, scooping up the rucksack before Cal could move. Bron put his hands to the wheels of the chair and turned it with an effort. "The gatekeeper here will show you your room. Relax, refresh yourself; you're my guest. A bell will ring for supper." Painfully, he wheeled himself away.

Cal followed the man up the great curving stairs and along a lavish corridor hung with red velvet. Forty pounds a night? No chance. The place was huge, maybe four star. And full, by the sound of it. They passed rows of closed doors; one was ajar and as they crossed the opening Cal saw a vast bed draped in crimson damask, tapestries hanging on the walls.

The gatekeeper was looking back. "This way, sir," he said. At the end of the corridor he opened a door and carried the rucksack inside, as carefully as if it was made of some precious metal. Cal stepped past him, amazed. A four-poster bed filled this room too, and as he turned he saw gilt mirrors and another log fire, and a small bathroom, its carpet deep and soft.

"Please ring if you need anything at all." The man made an elegant half-bow.

"Wait!" Cal turned. "Listen. Do I have to . . . dress up for supper?" He would have given anything not to have to ask.

"Not at all, sir. Come as you wish."

"And this place. Does it really belong to . . . Mr. Bron?"

"He is the King."

"Has he had some sort of accident?"

It was nosy, but the man didn't blink. Instead he looked grave. "The blow that struck him down devastated us all and all our lands and all the world. But I think you have given him—given us all—great hope. Will there be anything more?"

"No. Thanks." He had no idea what any of this meant. Were they that desperate for customers? For a confused moment he knew he should give some sort of tip, take a handful of coins out of his pocket like they did in films, and press something into the man's hand, but it would be too embarrassing and he didn't know how much and anyway, the man was gone.

Wearily, Cal went and sat on the bed, head in hands. He felt shaky and almost sick with hunger. And cut off, somehow, from everything, everyone, as if he'd stepped through some invisible barrier into a totally other place. He didn't belong here. But after a minute he made himself get up and go into the bathroom. The bath was huge; gold taps reflected his face. He turned the hot tap on and watched the water gush out, steaming. The roar of it cheered him. He'd always dreamed of staying in a luxury hotel. So why not make the best of it.

Later, warm and dry, wearing his favorite clothes—there had even been a little iron to get the creases out of his chinos—he sat by the roaring fire and leaned his head back in the comfortable chair. There was no minibar, but some hot sweetish drink with lemons in had been waiting on the table; he sipped it now, its warm fruity flavors. Slowly, he grinned. The station had been a nightmare, and the walk . . . well, all right, he'd got the creeps, but this—this was great. This was living. At home the flat would be empty like every night, and cold, because the two-bar electric fire would be off. There'd be no cooking smells, no TV. Only the old wooden clock in the dirty room, ticking. And next door's baby wailing.

No one could blame him for going. He'd had it since he was a kid, getting his own food, washing his own clothes, sorting himself out for school. It would do her good, anyway, to have to manage for a bit, to have to get herself together. It was over for him now. He was never going back. Never.

A sound made him look up. Repeated, it rang through the corridors and mysteries of the house. A sweet, silver bell.

✣ Three ✣

*Alas, that he asked no Question then! Even now I am cast
down on his account.*

Parzival

There were far more people in the place than he'd thought.
They came out of the rooms, thronging down the staircase,
chattering and laughing. One or two eyed him curiously.
They all seemed to know each other, and they were dressed
like something out of a James Bond film. The women wore
long gowns, sparkling with bits of feathers and fur and the
glitter of diamonds. Money. You could almost smell it. He
thought of all the designer names he'd heard of—these people
probably bought their stuff in places like that, in London,
those big, brightly-lit shops he'd seen in magazines. And the
men wore dress suits or uniforms, and talked loudly. He had
never felt so out of place.

The stairway was broad and curving; the carpet deep and

soft, a vivid scarlet. As the crowd pushed down around him he wondered for a bewildered second how they'd all got here; thought of the dark, tree-covered lane, the overgrown garden. But then, he must have come in the back way. There must be a car park at the front. A reception desk. This was some dinner dance for the local nobs.

He almost turned around then and went back up, but it would have been too hard to push through all those people, so he let them sweep him down and in through the double doors on the left, trailing behind a group of tall men, feeling lost and uneasy. Two boys with trays of drinks flanked the entrance; Cal took a glass and sipped it defiantly, not catching the boy's eye in case he was smirking. The pale liquid tasted of some delicate spice. It was definitely alcohol. He had a rule about not touching the stuff, because of what it did to his mother, but he could hardly pour it away here.

None of this was how he'd expected it. He'd stayed once in a bed-and-breakfast on a school trip, and then it had been small round tables in a dining room smelling of bacon and furniture polish, the landlady's tacky Spanish souvenirs on the walls. This was more like something from a film. Great swags of autumn fruits hung around the tables; the cloths were of gold and bronze damask, layered one on another, the whole chamber brilliant with candles. The smell of perfumes and the tantalizing sizzle of roasting meat made him swallow; he was almost dizzy with hunger.

People were sitting down. He had no idea where to go, so he stood awkwardly by a great bouquet of flowers, sipping nervously at the pale liquor. Should he just sit anywhere? But they all knew one another. The impulse to slip out and race upstairs was so strong he took a step back, straight into someone who gripped his elbow. "Excuse me, sir." It was one of the waiters. A boy taller than him, not much older, with a smooth face and shining blond hair. Cal disliked him on sight.

"What?" he said, pulling back.

"If you'd like to come this way."

Hot, Cal glared around. "Where?"

"The Fisher King sends his respects. He wants you to sit at his right this evening, sir. As his most honored guest."

Cal narrowed his eyes. "Are you winding me up?"

The boy didn't flicker. "I assure you, sire . . ."

"Don't mess with me or I'll deck you, party or not." Cal banged the glass down on a table; it toppled and spilled, the wine soaking the cloth. He scrubbed at it anxiously. A few people glanced around.

The tall boy looked pained, but from behind Cal a deep voice said, "Leave it, lad. I'll sort this."

Cal turned fast. The bouncer was hefty, and his beard was red. He was grinning. "I reckon you're more my sort than these lords and ladies," he said, his voice sly.

Cal shrugged. It was true but it annoyed him even more. "You were in the boat," he said.

"Right. And the lad was telling the truth. The King wants you." Putting a great hand on Cal's shoulder he turned him firmly, and Cal saw a long table at the top of the room, and the man called Bron sitting at its center, watching them between the arriving guests. Next to him was an empty chair.

"Do I have to?" Cal asked.

"Shy, are we?" The red-haired giant laughed, a bark of amusement. "Wouldn't have thought it, myself."

Cal stalked away from him icily.

Bron watched him come. "Is everything all right?"

Cal gripped the back of the empty chair. "Fine."

"You find my establishment a little strange."

"I feel bloody weird in it." Cal turned abruptly. "I'm sorry, but it's not the sort of place I'm used to. Maybe I should go and eat upstairs."

Bron's look was dark and hard. Then he said, "I would be glad, Cal, if you sat with me. It's very important to me. Please, do sit down."

Cal sighed, and pulled out the chair. Then he saw for the first time how ornate it was. Like a throne of some black, delicate stone. Strange letters were carved down its arms and across the back, and it was old too, because the red upholstery looked faded and yet unworn, as if no one ever sat there. On its back an osprey perched, a real one that blinked at him, unmoving. He hesitated. And maybe it was his imagination but the talk in the room faltered and seemed quieter, and some of the guests had turned to him and were watching. Bron looked away, his fingers pleating a fold of the tablecloth. For a moment Cal had the oddest reluctance to sit in the chair; he almost felt as if he would be committing himself to something. But the big guy stood behind Bron and smirked, and so he sat abruptly.

Perceptibly, the chatter in the room rose. Women laughed. People seemed relieved. Maybe Bron was too, because he nodded sharply up to the red-haired giant, who clapped his hands and, as if it was a signal, the waiters brought the food in.

It was a banquet. A feast. The courses were more elaborate than anything Cal had ever dreamed of, and they kept coming. Fish first, curls and delicately sauced bite-sized pieces of it, and though he disliked fish Cal was amazed at the variety of tastes. Tureens of hot, spicy meats were placed in front of him, and tiny exotic vegetables, and dips and dressings he didn't even know the names of. Between courses there were intricate little nothings of melt-in-the-mouth cheese and seafood and savory pastries, and a rich pâté dressed with peacock feathers, which he hoped wasn't peacock but might have been. Steamy puddings followed, creamy with honey, and cool confections of chocolate and coffee, and mounds of tangy citrus fruits too small to be oranges. Under his fingers the bread rolls broke open, white and soft: the piled cherries shone in the massed candlelight.

Cal ate everything. He was ravenous, and though he tried

to be cool about such abundance, the flavors were so amazing that he attacked everything steadily, until his belt felt tight and he was hot and slightly woozy with the pale white wine Bron poured for him.

The dark man spoke little, and ate less. He pushed the small portions around his plate, listening restlessly to the musicians in the gallery somewhere above playing dreamy melodies of flute and harp. Behind him his giant servant stood, arms folded, attentive. Once when Bron coughed and reached for water the big man had it there instantly, his cheery face clouded. Bron sipped it, and sat back. "Thank you, Leo," he murmured. He looked pale with fever.

Cal put his spoon down in the empty syllabub dish and Bron almost smiled. "You enjoyed it."

"It was fantastic!" He picked up the heavy crystal glass, turning it so the rainbow facets glinted. "All of it. If you knew what sort of place I live in . . ." He stopped abruptly. Never talk about home. Never. It was one of his rules.

Carefully, as if some moment had come, Bron laid his own fork down and looked out at the crowded tables. "We all have our hidden pain, Cal. We've all been wounded."

"Not me," he said recklessly. "I've walked away."

"You're lucky." Bron gave him a strange glance. "I could have said that once but not now. I can never walk anywhere again." His face was drawn, his skin clammy. In that brilliant room the dark clothes he wore seemed out of place, even though they were rich velvets and glinted here and there with discreet emeralds. He leaned forward for a moment and held the table's edge with an indrawn breath that was unmistakably pain. The osprey screeched, pecking at its harness. Cal looked around hastily, but the big man had gone. "Are you all right? Can I get someone?"

"I am as well as I can be." Bron tried to pour water but the jug shook in his long frail fingers, so Cal took it and poured. The man sipped, his eyes, a deep green to match the jewels on his coat, closed and hidden. Then he rubbed his forehead with one palm, pushing up his dark hair. "Cal, listen to me. I wasn't born like this. Do you know how it is to have a wound that will not heal, a torment of pain? To want to die and not be able to? I think you might know something of that, or you would not be here."

"Not me," Cal interrupted quickly. He felt embarrassed. He hated illness in any form and the wine was making him feel bold and harsh; he looked away and said, "Can't the doctors do anything?"

Bron stopped. He seemed tense. He said, in a quieter voice, "There may be one cure."

"Then go for it. You've got money. Go private. Money can get you anything."

"Can it?" The King's green eyes were watching him. "You believe that?"

"I'd like the chance to find out. Yes, I do. Why not?"

Bron frowned wryly. "Maybe I thought that once." He held out a coiled piece of fish; the osprey snatched it greedily. "I cannot walk, Cal, or ride or hunt, and because of that I amuse myself by fishing. Leo carries me down to the boat, and we row out onto the lake, under the moon. How cool it is there, and the waves lap so calmly. And we fish. All the silver, teeming life of the lake comes into our nets, big and small, good and evil. Many we throw back. Some we bring here, to the Castle. And Leo jokes that one night we might catch a real treasure, a great fish with a ring in its belly as in the old stories." He glanced at Cal, sidelong. "Maybe tonight we did."

Cal drank. The wine was blurring his eyesight; he felt dizzy and awkward. He wasn't sure what all this was getting at. Maybe now he'd eaten he could make some excuse and get to bed.

"Where were you going," Bron asked quietly, "on the train?"

"To live with my uncle."

"For good?"

"Too right."

"Your mother will miss you."

"She'll get by."

"And your father?"

It was against his rules to answer but something made him say, "My father walked out when I was two." He shrugged, watching the candles, how they put themselves out, one by one. "I don't know why I'm telling you this anyway. She doesn't care. Not really. She drinks. Says she hears voices. Now she can get on without me."

"And will she?"

"I'm past caring." Grimly, Cal filled his glass and drank again. It was the music that was doing it. The music had turned into a fog; it was winding down from the gallery and was snuffing all the candles out with deft gray fingers. Even the great fire that had roared in the hearth behind them was sinking, clouding over. The clatter of knives and forks, the chatter of the guests, was fading under the weight of it, an obscurity in the room, a gathering mist. Someone was turning down the world's volume.

Cal tugged at his collar. "It's hot in here."

Bron's fingers were white on the wineglass. "Cal, I need you to help. You must . . ." He stopped abruptly, then turned and said with sudden desperation, "This agony runs through all my realm. The kingdom is laid waste. You can heal it. If you went back . . ."

"Back?" In front of Cal three candles winked out; he stared at them in bewilderment. "Back where?"

"Home."

He stared at the man in amazement, his narrow, oddly familiar face. Then he stood up. "No chance!"

Bron swiveled his wheeled chair with his bony hands. He

seemed consumed with a secret torment. "Please. The Grail is coming. Only see it. Look at it. Do what you can to help us."

And the music stopped. It stopped instantly, like a CD switched off in midnote. The room was black. All the people had gone. Cal swallowed; for a second he knew he was somewhere lost, a palace nowhere in the world, deep in darkness, and then the doors opened, and a boy came in. He was one of the tall, fair-haired ones from the door, and he carried what looked to be a long rod, upright in both hands. He walked across the room quickly, without looking at Cal, and Cal stared, stunned at what the wine had done to his eyes. Because this was no rod, but a spear. *And the spear was bleeding.* Slowly, horribly, a great globule of blood welled from its tip; it ran down, trickling stickily over the boy's fingers, down the rough shaft, dripping in dark splashes on the wooden floor.

Cal felt sick. "This is crazy," he whispered.

Behind the boy came two more, each carrying a branched golden candlestick, and the candles that burned in them seemed to have such light that it made Cal bring his hands together and clench them on the table. Beside him, he sensed Bron's rigid pain.

The doorway was empty. But something else was coming. Something so inexplicable, so terrible that it made the very air shiver, a sudden breath of icy purity, so that Cal stepped right back without knowing it, shocked into fear. Sweat chilled on his spine, the very darkness in the doorway seeming to crackle and swell as if the room breathed in, all the curtains flapping, the casements gusting open with terrifying cracks. He caught the edge of the table.

She had times like these. She'd see things, she'd scream, clutch her ears. How many times had he phoned the hospital, got a taxi, got her to Casualty. As if her head was bursting with visions, she'd say. Visions and angels. As if they were all in there with her.

A girl came in. She was taller than the boys, and her hair was fair and her dress green. She carried a cup. She carried it carefully, as if it was precious, and he could see how ancient it was, how dented and scarred, and that it was gold, and there were jewels in its rim. For a moment he could see, but it shone, it shone so fiercely it almost burned and quivered in her hands, and he wondered how she could bear it, how he could bear to see it. Because it burned him too, in his eyes until he closed them and then like a heat and glow against his body, and yet none of it was real, none of it existed, he had to remember that.

Bron's fingers were tight on his arm.

There was another room. There had been no door before, but there was now, and the boys with the spear and the candlesticks walked in there, and the girl did too, and as she passed she raised her face from the glory of the Grail and gave Cal one look, quick and rapt. And he was seared with the sudden joy of it, the nameless, unbelievable joy, but the door swung shut and the light was gone and the music was back. As if it had never stopped.

Knives and forks clattered. Glasses tinkled. All the candles glimmered. Cal rubbed his hand weakly down his face. He felt shaky, his whole body was wet with sweat. He collapsed into the chair.

"Cal?"

He turned. Bron was watching him, eyes bright, and behind him the red-bearded man waited, and the osprey stared, hawk-sharp.

"Did you see?"

"See?"

"You must ask me about it, Cal." Bron's grip was so tight it hurt. "You must ask me. That's all you need to do. Ask me about what you saw."

Cal shook him off, shivering. "Leave me alone. I've got to get out."

"But you saw! You must have seen."

Dully, Cal licked his lips, obstinate. He wasn't drunk. He wouldn't be like her. Never. He'd sworn long ago he'd never be like her. *"I didn't see a thing,"* he whispered.

Bron looked as though someone had struck him. For a moment his disappointment was so terrible Cal felt worse, chilled with terror. "Could I have some water?" he croaked. The big man poured it and pushed it over with a look of disgust. The coldness was wonderful in his seared throat. Putting the glass down he breathed out and said clearly and bitterly, "Either you or I are drunk, your majesty."

Leo had both his hands on Bron's shoulders. When the dark man looked up he seemed haunted, more haggard, as if an eternity of pain had fallen on him. There was a grim despair in his face. "I should have known," he whispered.

✢ Four ✢

And near to the gate the vegetation was taller than elsewhere.

Peredur

His head hurt. The dull ache came prodding down through layers and layers of sleep; it was an annoying throb, a knocking in his temples and throat. Cal groaned and rolled over, dragging the coarse blanket over his head. But the pain wouldn't let him go. He lay there, awake, eyes tightly closed. For a moment he thought he was at home, tense in the bed, listening for the old noises downstairs, but then he remembered and let his body relax. Though the room seemed oddly cold.

He had come up to bed straight after the meal, had said a shame-faced good night to Bron and the dark-haired man had nodded bitterly. "Good-bye Cal. It will be a long journey, as I feared."

He remembered the osprey's yellow eyes, round and fierce. It was as if they had expected something great of him, as if he had failed them. But he'd drunk too much—he must have done. Because spears didn't bleed and there was no light in the world like that which had scorched from the battered, golden cup. It had been some normal thing, people carrying dishes, and he'd seen it all wrong.

He shivered. He'd heard her going on about things like this. Maybe it was schizophrenia, psychosis, one of those terrible words he'd looked up in the reference library that hot endless weekend she'd been in the hospital. He knew it was in his blood, in him. Maybe this was the start of it.

Terrified, he sat up. Ignoring the headache he groped in the dimness for the marble bedside lamp with its ornate tassels, but he couldn't find it, so he pulled the blankets aside and slid out of bed. The floor felt oddly rough under his bare feet. He padded across and drew the curtains. Then he turned, and stared in amazement. Where was the room? The beautiful, glossy magazine furnishings? *What was happening to him?*

He saw a small stark cell, the walls plain and gray, with vast black stars in places where whole lumps of plaster had cracked and fallen off. On the rough planks of the floor old straw was scattered, and there were bones in it, gnawed and yellow.

Cal sidestepped in disgust. "God," he whispered.

His rucksack was propped against the door. The ceiling

was high, green and dripping with damp. The curtains were rags and the bed a simple wooden frame with a gray mattress and the filthiest blanket he had ever seen lying crumpled on it. And it was bitterly cold.

He turned fast, as something spoke behind him, but the window was cracked and only the wind whispered in its corner, high-pitched in the green ivy. Cal put his hands up slowly to the vibrating pane. Outside, through the flapping leaves, was the garden. Wet, dripping, overgrown. A waste land.

Instantly he turned, grabbed his clothes, and struggled into them frantically. He had to get out! Either this was a madhouse, or it was him. He didn't want to talk to Bron, or the big man, or any of them. He just had to get back into the real world.

And then he saw the sword. He froze, one arm in his shirt. In the silence his heart thudded. It was a narrow blade, and it looked wickedly sharp. Small crystals of ice glinted on its edge. It had been thrust through the pillow and into the wooden headboard, hard. Just above where his head must have been.

Suddenly weak, Cal sat on the bed. Finally, warily, he reached out and took hold of the corded handle of the weapon. It fitted his hand perfectly, and he felt the icy metal slowly warm against his fingers. He pulled, then again, hard, and the sword came out.

It was a beautiful thing. The pommel and guard were of

steel, chased with intricate patterns and small red garnets, and down the blade a ripplework of beaten metal reflected his face with cold precision. He touched the cutting edge carefully, his breath clouding the steel.

There was a stiff piece of parchment on the pillow; the sword had pinned it there. He picked it up reluctantly and read: *My parting gift to you. Take it. It will serve you as you have served me. Go with God.* It was signed, in a jagged scrawl: *Bron.*

Cal sat silent. He had no idea what to do. "What the hell do I want with a sword?" he muttered aloud, and as if in response a drip of water fell from the ceiling and trickled down the blade. It broke the spell. He jammed the paper in his pocket, and the sword, roughly, in the mesh at the back of the rucksack. He'd leave it on the table downstairs. He had enough to worry about.

The corridor was deserted. It smelled of damp and neglect, and the carpet was gone. As he walked quickly along it his footsteps echoed, and when he came to the stairs his worst fears lay before him. The curved banister was the same, but it led down into desolation. There was no fire, no table, no chandeliers. The hall was a ruin, the roof long fallen, ivy growing inside all the walls. Cal came down and stood on the bottom step and looked at it, fear clenched in his stomach like an agony. He knew what he had seen last night. And it hadn't been this.

Suddenly panic-stricken, he jumped down into the rubble of bricks and plaster and shoved the great doors wide to the banqueting room. The gilt ceiling lay in pieces on the floor; black mildew coated the walls. A great thicket of weeds grew out of the chimney. He pushed his way in. The tables were gone, the luxurious feast, the dishes, the guests, the shining cup. None of it was here. He must really be crazy. Except that the sword clinked reassuringly at his back.

And there was no door.

It was only a small thing among all the betrayal of his senses but it caught his curiosity through the fear and bewilderment. The spear and candles and the golden cup had been taken across this room and through a door. The room was the same—ruined and aged, but the same. But there was not, and never could have been, a door. He could see the brickwork through the buckled gilt panels. If he climbed over there he could even put his hands on it.

Quickly he turned, scrambled back across the hall, and found the entrance he had come in through the night before. The glass panels of knights and horsemen had long since fallen in; ivy choked the porch so thoroughly he had to grope for the bolts in a green, musty dimness and then shove and shudder the whole warped door to get it wide enough for him to slip through. Even then the ivy was too thick, a dusty smothering curtain, stinking of damp. After a moment he pulled the sword out and sliced through the woody stems; he found he could slash an opening, force his way out, and as he surfaced from the leaves the gray daylight was cool, and he breathed it deep. But the rotting garden made him think again of that old story, the prince, the sleeping castle. It wasn't supposed to end like this. This was all the wrong way around.

It was hard to get out. Great umbels of hogweed had grown down the path and he had to snap through them, seed drifting in his face, and the statues of bears and foxes were fallen or lost in swaths of bramble, decades of growth that snagged him and barred his way. He had to cut a tunnel and edge through, crouching, furious at the torn scags of his clothes.

At the gate in the wall the latch was broken; the outer door banged in the wind. He pushed through it and looked up. There was a rusty bracket. But no hotel sign.

For a moment he stood there in the pattering rain with the sword dripping in his hand. The castle was a shadow behind its tangled wilderness, silent, without even birdsong. There was no one here.

He had meant to toss the sword back inside; instead he found himself pushing it into the rucksack. Then he turned. When he spoke his voice was bitter. "I'm sorry. It's not me you need. I don't even know what you want me to do."

Rain dripped. And the wind whipped the door out of his numb fingers and slammed it in his face.

✦ ✦ ✦

The tramp to the station seemed endless; after half an hour he was soaked and thirsty. The lanes were dripping and muddy with dead leaves, the ditches overflowing, all hedgerows bare. He had a sudden terror that too much time had passed; that the night in the castle had been weeks out here, and it almost made him run in panic, but the rucksack was too heavy and he had to stop, breathless. Stupid. Calm down. And the lane was different. He hadn't remembered any turnings last night but they were here now, and around the next bend the lane divided into two, with no signposts, the fields silent but for a few cows that chewed and watched him. Far off, a flock of rooks rose noisily from some trees. Cal chose the left-hand lane, and walked on, soaked and hopeless.

Until he heard the car. It was a long way back but it was coming up fast behind him, and he turned quickly, waiting. A Range Rover. Smart. He flagged it down. A middle-aged man put his head out of the window dubiously.

"I'm looking for the station," Cal said quickly, trying not to seem so wet.

"Station?"

"Railway station. Corbenic."

"Never heard of it." The man pulled his head in and spoke to his wife. A small Yorkshire terrier yipped in the back.

"There's a station at Ludlow." The man looked him up and down; Cal felt hot with humiliation. "We're going near it. Would you like a lift?"

"Thanks!"

The car was gloriously warm, and smelled of leather and cigarettes. The dog sniffed him once and then jumped down, scrambling into the front on the woman's lap. Her manicured fingers caressed its silky hair. "Terrible weather," she said.

"Yes . . ." Cal watched the rain run from his soaked trousers and darken the seat; he moved his coat to cover it. "I think I must have gotten lost."

"Come far?"

"From the Castle Hotel." He said it deliberately, knowing only too well that the man would answer as he did.

"Don't know it." He changed gear. "What was that place again?"

"Corbenic."

"We've lived here for three years and I don't think I've even heard the name before." The woman turned and smiled over her shoulder pleasantly. Then the smile froze to a sickly rigidity. She had seen the sword. Cal swore silently. It was jutting out from the rucksack, the blade bright in the watery daylight. She turned back to the front quickly, then flashed a terrified glance at him in the mirror. Cal stared grimly out of the window. Maybe he should say something. Explain. Lie. The woman nudged her husband. Now he kept looking up in the mirror. The car veered. It was going too fast.

Suddenly Cal couldn't care less what sort of weirdo they thought he was. He leaned back and pulled the wet coat around him, brooding, glad he'd scared them. Why did he always have to be worried about what people thought of him? Why was he always so anxious?

They came to a crossing; the red light stopped them. The driver's gloved fingers tapped feverishly on the padded wheel. "Got far to go then?" His voice was false with cheeriness.

"Chepstow."

"Nice place." They were terrified of him. He smiled coldly. The man put his foot down and drove, before the lights changed. Right, left, through some streets of small black and white houses. Then he pulled up jerkily. "This is it."

Cal opened the door, got out, and heaved the rucksack after him. In the mirrors their scared eyes watched. He couldn't stand it. It was stupid but it mattered to him. He put his hand on the sword hilt and grinned foolishly. "Historical stuff. Sort of a hobby, really."

The Yorkie barked.

"Right," the driver said. Relief was all over him like sweat. "Got you." Then the door slammed, and the Range Rover roared away.

On the tarmac, despising himself, Cal looked down at the blade, then whipped his jacket off viciously and wrapped the thing in it, tight. The sharp edge took a tiny treacherous slice out of his finger; blood splashed in sudden drops on his shirt. Furious, he shoved the sword under one arm. *It will serve you,* the note had said, *as you have served me.*

✣ Five ✣

Perfect was Gweir's prison in the courts of the Otherworld.

Spoils of Annwn

"Of course, I'll be expecting you to pay rent. It doesn't have to be much, in the beginning, but the principle is important, Cal. You've left home. You'll have to pay your way from now on." It was hardly much of a welcome. Trevor dumped the rucksack in the car truck. He was a small man, meticulously neat, his coat dark over the business suit. "I'm glad you're not loaded down with stuff," he said, dusting his hands. "I hate the place cluttered."

"Not much to bring," Cal muttered.

He was weary. The journey from Ludlow had been a nightmare. Waiting ages, then having to buy a new ticket because his had been for yesterday, then missing the connection at Newport. He wanted to moan about it but his uncle

didn't even ask, just sat in beside him and looked at him.
"You're taller." His gaze settled on Cal's crumpled shirt, the
cheap, useless jacket. Saying nothing, not needing to say it,
he turned and started the car.

They drove down through the steep, narrow streets of the
small town, through the arch in the old walls. Afternoon
shoppers were few on the pavements; across the housetops
fading bunting flapped in the rain. The shops were small.
Smaller even than Bangor. Cal sighed.

"So what was it like?" Trevor asked.

"Sorry?"

"The hotel. What sort of bill am I going to get?"

Cal pulled a tiny thread off the cuff of his shirt. "None."

His uncle looked at him quickly. "Come into money?"

"I've been saving. A long time."

Trevor nodded. "I'm glad to hear it. Still got that account I
started for you?"

"Yes." It had been their secret. His mother had never
known, because if she had she would have had the money
out, wasted it, drunk it away, and it was his. All the savings
from his weekend job had gone in there, every penny. For
months now he had waited eagerly for every statement,
watching how the tiny amounts of interest had been added
on. He'd even gone without food sometimes, if she'd given
him anything for a takeaway, just to have the pleasure of
adding to it. A secret, vivid pleasure.

"I rang Annie last night." Trevor turned the wheel; the car went around the traffic circle and climbed the hill. His lips were tight with distaste. "To be honest, I don't think she took in a word I was saying. 'Where's Cal?' she kept asking. As if she was expecting you home for tea. She does know, doesn't she, that this is for good?"

"I'm sick of telling her." Cal watched the houses pass grimly.

"And that medication she's on, is it any use?"

"When she takes it." He didn't want to think about her. Not now. He didn't want the shadow of her to spoil this. The car had turned into a quiet cul-de-sac called Otter's Brook, lined with houses. New, expensive houses. Cal looked at them with satisfaction, and a sort of pride. They were detached, double-glazed, well-cared for. Some had double garages. A new kid's bike lay in the drive of one, right out in the open, as if it was safe to do that here. Big cars were parked by immaculate green lawns.

Trevor reversed the car into a sloping driveway lined with terracotta pots and pulled up carefully. "This is it. I'll let you in, and then I'll have to get back to the office. You can make yourself at home."

Cal bundled the jacket under one arm, carefully rewrapping the sword's dangerous blade. He wished he'd left the hateful thing behind. But somehow it was important. It was his sanity; the only thing that proved that Corbenic had been real.

He waited while Trevor unlocked the white door with its gleaming brass knocker, enjoying the quiet. God, this place was so different. Another world. In Sutton Street, right now, a disused stove rusted outside number eight, and the doors would all be open; music would be blaring from somewhere, and tonight there'd be all the usual fights, kids on street corners, new graffiti on the walls. But not here. This was quiet. Detached. He said the word to himself, as if he savored it.

"I'll just go and check there's enough milk." Trevor went quickly into the kitchen, and Cal dumped his rucksack on the spotless cream carpet and stood there, arms full of wrapped sword.

This was it. This was what he'd dreamed of. There were a few magazines at home, glossy, *Homes and Gardens.* His mother had kept them; sometimes, on her good days, she'd get them out and sit there, among all the mess, flicking the pages, smoking nonstop. "One day, Cal," she'd say, over the exquisitely tasteful rooms. "One day this'll be us." Maybe when he was a kid he had believed her. But not now. Not for years.

Yet here it was. Sofas of softest cream leather, paintings, delicate curtains, big arty-looking vases. A huge, open-plan room, nothing out of place. Warm. Clean. His uncle's computer on an ebony desk. Television. State-of-the-art sound system. Leatherbound books, all matching. He even felt classier as he looked at it.

"Right." Trevor came in, gave the rucksack the briefest flicker of annoyance and rubbed his small hands together nervously. "Your bedroom is the one at the back. Have a shower, get yourself something to eat. I'll be back a bit late, and Thérèse will be coming at about eight; we're going out for supper. So I'm afraid you'll have the place to yourself tonight."

"No problem." Cal picked the rucksack up, awkward.

"Cal." Halfway out of the door his uncle paused. He didn't turn, but spoke to Cal through the chrome-edged mirror. "A few ground rules. No mess. No drugs. No smoking. No fights. No friends—of either gender—back here without asking me. You wash up what you use, look after your own clothes, shop for any food you want." He pulled an odd, apologetic face. "Though I'm sure you've been doing that for a long time now."

Cal shrugged. They both knew that.

"It's just . . . It's a big thing I'm doing here for you. Getting you this job. Having you in my house. A risk. Don't let me down, Cal."

"You won't even know I'm here," Cal said drily. He knew a threat when he heard it. "Do you think I'm going to jeopardize all this?"

Trevor shook his head, half-smiling. "No, I don't. You're like me, I know that. But this is my place, Cal, that's all. I'll see you about six then."

After the car had pulled away Cal stood in the room, listening to its silence, smelling the faint leathery, soapy smells of the house. In the quiet the fridge hummed. Then he kicked his boots off and crossed the immaculate carpet. He wanted to dump the sword but nowhere seemed right. Through the first door was a kitchen, just as spick-and-span, obviously barely used. A chrome espresso machine—at least that's what he thought it was—had a postcard propped against it, a photo of some vineyard, with a French stamp. *See you Friday*, it said. *Brought us a good vintage. Thérèse.*

For a second as he put the card down Cal knew he was in a place as alien to him as the castle of Corbenic, if not more so. Then the feeling was gone, and he looked for the stairs. They were open-plan, blond wood. A great skylight let a shaft of sunlight down on him as he found the back bedroom and went in. The walls, like all those in the house, were palest cream, with an abstract print of some blotches of orange and green. The carpet was charcoal gray, and the bed had a black-and-white striped duvet. He sat on it slowly. There was a fitted cupboard, which he jumped up and opened. It was empty, but for a neat row of hangers. Cal grinned. At home a whole pile of junk and dirty washing would have tumbled out.

He remembered the sword suddenly and crouched, kneeling, tipping it out of his jacket and shoving it far under the bed, right under because it didn't fit in this place, didn't belong. But even when he stood up again he knew it was there, a blot on this perfection. He'd sell it. The thought made him laugh aloud; then he went to the window and drew aside the delicate lace curtains.

The estate was hushed. Birds sang. A car purred softly down the hill. No one passed by, no one. The houses were all new, every garden tended, every errant leaf carefully swept up. Beyond he could see a line of forestry toward Tintern, deep, green wooded slopes. And the castle.

He stared at it almost in dismay. For a moment his fingers were tight on the curtain; then he took a deep breath and made himself smile. It wasn't the same. It was Chepstow Castle of course, a Norman ruin on the clifftop, a gaunt gray mass of roofless towers and halls. He'd seen it from the train. It was open to the public. It wasn't the same. Still, it annoyed him. It was old, and broken. It spoiled his view.

He showered and changed in the pristine bathroom and cleaned up carefully afterward, hanging his clothes meticulously, putting his few shirts into the empty drawers, every color separate, then made himself coffee and some sandwiches and took them into the huge room, switching the lamps on and drawing the curtains on the sudden November twilight. Almost reluctantly he sat on the leather sofa; it was so soft he almost spilled the cup and he swore, and then grinned.

There were plenty of CDs; he flicked through them

and pulled a face. Sinatra, jazz, middle-of-the-road stuff. Thick square candles lined the fire surround. They'd never been lit.

On the table next to him was a gray, slim phone. He looked at it for a long time, sipping the coffee; even when the cup was empty it was an effort for him to put it down, and reach over and pick the phone up. The dialing tone purred reassuringly. He dialed the number. She took a long time to answer; he almost put it down in relief but then the familiar voice said, "Cal? Is that you?" She was bad. He knew that right away, just from the quaver in her voice.

"Hi," he said quietly.

"Oh God, Cal, where are you? Where have you been? Trevor said . . ."

"I'm all right." He felt it creeping back on him already, the impatience, the irritation. "I had to stop in a hotel last night. I'm here now, at Trevor's." He glanced around. "It's really nice."

She giggled meaninglessly. "You're coming back, aren't you? I forget when. . . ."

"I told you. I'm getting a job here. At Trevor's office. I told you."

"The bin's full," she said hopelessly. "How do I empty it? And last night, Cal, the voices were in my room. I heard them, they were in the chimney and they were telling that story again. . . ."

His fingers were tight on the phone. "Have you taken your pills?"

"Pills? Which ones?"

"The blue ones. Remember? The ones Doctor Lewis said . . ."

"Oh, I've taken them. All of them."

"ALL of them?" For a second his heart thudded. "What do you mean, all of them?"

"Haven't I? I thought I had. The story was the one about the bed, Cal, and if you lay in the bed the voices come there too, and there are curtains round it, and a sword in the pillow."

"What?" he said quickly, but she went on without stopping, and it was the same as always, the breathless, meaningless stories and he was barely listening, his skin crawling with nerves. She did this to him. She always did this. Then, somewhere behind it all there was a voice, calling. "Who's that?" he said instantly.

She stopped, confused. "What? What do I do about the bin?"

"Put it out for the men. On Thursday." He was panicky; suddenly the image of the overflowing dustbin made him sweat. He should have sorted it before he came, but then it would be like that every week now, wouldn't it, and he couldn't stay there anymore, he couldn't stand it.

"Are you coming back?" she whispered, as if she'd heard.

"In a few weeks. For the weekend. I promise. Who's there

with you?" It might be some man. But she said, "Sally." Relief flooded him. "Put her on, will you."

"I love you, Cal."

He nodded grimly. "Put Sally on, Mam, please."

There was a crackle, a clatter. Then Sally said, "Hi, Cal."

"Is she all right?" he asked, numb.

"Not so good. She came banging on the door early hours of this morning so I came in and got her to bed. She'd been down the pub."

"Sorry," he said, the misery so heavy all at once he felt sick.

"Not your fault." He could imagine Sally sitting on the table, her ample bottom in the jogging trousers.

"Make sure she takes the pills, Sal. The blue ones. Please. And don't forget the appointment with the psychiatrist on Monday."

"Don't you worry." Sal's voice was quieter. "Don't fret, Cal. Don't torment yourself. This is a chance for you, love, maybe the only chance you'll ever have to get on, so don't ruin it. I'll keep an eye on Annie. Give me the number and I'll ring you tomorrow."

He gave it, and said, "I couldn't have done this without you."

"When you're making wads of cash you can pay me back." Her voice turned, then came back. "Do you want to say good night to your mam? She's gone off somewhere."

"No," he said quickly. "It'll just upset her again."

"I'll find those pills. Good night, Cal."

He put the phone down, and found he was sweating. As if he'd run for miles and miles. In the warm, still room he felt exhausted, and it was true, he had run, hadn't he; run away and left her to fend for herself, though everyone knew she couldn't. And it was illness, it wasn't her fault, not really. But he couldn't take it anymore, and he wouldn't think about it, because Sally lived down the road and it'd be all right. And he wouldn't think about Corbenic, either, because that was in him, that was worse.

So he washed up, and when Trevor came home he said hello to Thérèse, who turned out to be as well dressed and elegant as he'd thought she would, her voice faintly accented. French, maybe. Waiting for Trevor, she perched on the edge of the sofa. "So. You'll be working at the accountants'?"

"Four days a week. On Wednesdays I have to go to college. For a course."

She smiled, her dark hair gleaming. A faint scent of perfume drifted from her. "Is that what you want?" she asked.

"Yes," he said, surprised.

She nodded kindly. "That's good then. That you know what you want."

When they'd gone he watched television all night, a meaningless babble of programs and then went up and lay in the comfort of the black-and-white bed, one lamp throwing soft shadows on the ceiling. It was beautifully, wonderfully silent. No baby crying through the walls. No lying awake wondering what time his mother would come in. But he did lie awake, wondering just that, for a long time.

✠ Six ✠

"Alas that I have you in my sight," she said,
"since you failed so completely."

Parzival

It was the quiet he couldn't get used to. He stared out of the window at the cul-de-sac; even on a Saturday morning it was deserted, except for one man washing his car a few doors down. "They don't live so much outside here," he said quietly. "It's all indoors."

"And that's how I like it." Trevor turned a page of the *Financial Times* and poured another glass of orange juice. Freshly squeezed, of course. He sipped it. "Some of them I've never even seen. It's just a dormitory really."

"How long have you lived here?"

"Five years. Since it was built." He looked up, and in the shiny reflection of the window Cal saw that his face was amused. "I couldn't get to grips with it either, when I first moved out. No one bothering you. You think it's normal, all that living in each other's pockets, all that rubbish and dog muck on the streets, the boarded windows, the burned-out cars. Knowing what places not to go, who's buying, who's selling, whose eyes not to meet." He chuckled, but Cal couldn't even smile. "God, I couldn't believe how different things were here. It was like a weight off my shoulders." For a second then, an odd haunted look came into his eyes. He glanced down at the paper quickly. "It'll be the same for you."

Cal nodded. It was true. He realized that he could walk down to the town right now and no one—*no one*—would know him. He could do exactly what he liked. He was free. It made him restless; he turned. "Thought I'd go for a walk. Explore."

Trevor looked slightly relieved, but just nodded. "Fine. I'm at the office till twelve, then golf. The day's yours. You may as well enjoy it. Work starts on Monday."

As he pulled on his jacket upstairs, Cal grinned to himself. He'd break his rules and buy a few things. Batteries for the Walkman. Maybe some new music. It was a day to celebrate. And he'd find the bank and see about having his account moved down here. For a second he remembered the sword and frowned. There must be a junk shop somewhere. Or antiques. He had a vivid image of himself chatting confidently with an impressed shop owner, being told the sword was worth thousands. Well, it might make a bit. He'd find out.

As he walked down the hill between the open-plan gardens he felt calm. The sunshine was warm on the clean pavements, and the few leaves still on the cherry trees were gloriously red and gold. He felt so happy he even let himself think about Corbenic. That brought the shadows back.

He couldn't explain anything of what had happened. Bron's banquet had been real, but had anyone else seen the strange cup or the bleeding lance, or felt that terrible, devastating longing, that pure joy? And in the morning it had all been ruined. As if there were layers of reality, one inside the other like an onion, and he'd peeled off two, by mistake. The only other explanation—the one Trevor would give—was that he'd been drunk, or had somehow arrived at the ruined castle and dreamed it all. But he hadn't. The sword proved that. And the note, but he'd lost the note. He must have dropped it in the scramble through the neglected garden, but he could remember exactly what it had said. It made him shiver; brought a sudden bitter coldness into his joy. Why did nothing ever go right? What was wrong with him?

Down at the bottom of the road the new houses faded out; he crossed into a street of older properties, and he had no idea where he was, so he followed it, as if walking anywhere would make him forget. And at the end of the street he found the town center.

Chepstow was old, and steep. The main street ran downhill, a haphazard tumble of shops and cafés and banks and a post office, splitting into little side streets so narrow they were more like alleys, with tiny dingy-looking pubs jutting onto the pavements, their blackboards chalked with the soup of the day or the chef's special. He wandered down. He knew that right at the bottom was the river, and the bridge that crossed into England, and the castle, guarding the crossing, but he didn't really want to go that far. Because it was a Saturday the place was busy; he drifted around charity shops and looked idly in window displays and the sun was almost warm and his happiness came quietly back.

He went to the bank and sat at a desk filling in a form, being called sir and enjoying it. In Woolworth's he bought batteries and looked at new CDs, because he couldn't listen to Trevor's stuff, but they were expensive and there was nothing he particularly wanted. In the town's only department store he wandered into the coffee shop and bought an espresso and sat in a corner sipping it, with a family opposite, the boy and girl laughing and drinking Coke, all four of them well scrubbed and well spoken and looking like something from an advertisement.

Tearing open the thin tube of sugar he felt lonely all at once. The woman—the kids' mother—had caught his glance and he looked away in case she guessed. He stirred the dark liquid and sipped it, though it was too hot. He'd have to get some friends. But kids of his age wouldn't be here. They'd be in the pubs and fast-food places. Cal scowled. He hated burgers. They reminded him of home. Anyway, kids of his age weren't much like him, he knew that only too well. He wanted good clothes, classy food. There wasn't anyone, really, much like him.

He put the empty cup down and looked up. There was a girl watching him. She was out in the department beyond the glass door. Curtains, bedding, that sort of thing.

Cal looked away, slightly hot. He tried to sit as if he was relaxed and highly confident, but he felt self-conscious, and couldn't help glancing over again.

She'd gone. No. Moved. Nearer the door. But she was looking at him. A sharp, intent look, as if she knew him, and there was something about her . . .

And in an instant he recognized her, a shock of fear and vivid joy. She had been in Corbenic. *She had carried the golden cup.*

He jumped up, making the crockery topple with a clink. People turned, but he was already elbowing his way through the crowded tables.

"Hey! Excuse me!" A large, slightly grim waitress barred his way. "That'll be one twenty, thank you."

One twenty! It was extortionate! But he slapped the coins into her palm and she stood back with a sarcastic smile, and he knew she thought he'd been trying to slip off without paying. He wouldn't care. He had to find the girl.

There were racks of curtains, billowing in the air-conditioning.

Gauzy fabrics rippled; he ran down the aisles of them but always the movement seemed to be somewhere else, on the other side. She was there, he knew. Dodging through he came to beds, rows of them, and far down at the end a figure slipped out between them.

"Wait!" he called. Pushing past a salesman he raced after her. Outside, somewhere very close, a clock was chiming, loud, like a church, nine, ten, eleven, and the noise almost seemed to obstruct him, to thicken the air, as he turned sideways to edge past women with loaded bags and a bored man with a stroller. Men's wear! She wouldn't be here! But there she was, a slight figure beside a counter of folded pullovers, watching him, her eyes bright. She wore a green dress. The same dress.

Cal cursed. He stood still and told himself he wouldn't take another step; he'd turn and find the door and get out of the shop into the sunshine. Then he was running. Through lingerie and children's wear and home furnishings and books she was always ahead, just out of sight. The clock struck, booming through the building. Surely it shouldn't be that loud! He found stairs and jumped down them, into a dim basement full of shining kitchen appliances.

Abruptly, the chimes stopped. Breathless, he looked around. No one else seemed to be down here. Small echoes shifted.

"It is you, isn't it?" he said quietly. In the dusty silence his words seemed to hang; he said desperately, "I just want to talk to you! About Corbenic."

No answer.

He took a step forward. In all the kettles and jugs and teapots; in the stainless steel coffee pots and toasters and mixers and drying racks he saw himself move, swollen and distorted and stretched and tiny. His mouth warped in the convex surfaces. "Please," he whispered.

She was there. Reflected. He turned quickly, but he couldn't find her. Only her reflections watched him, her eyes severe in the dimness.

"How could you let us down like that?" Her whisper was intense and fierce, and it startled him.

"What?"

"You lied! To Bron, to yourself. You saw the Grail . . ."

"That cup!"

"Yes. That cup. And the spear. You saw the door open. And you denied all of it!"

Cal stared at her face, twisted in the shiny handle of a kettle. In milk jugs and sugar basins she watched him, seeming young and then old, warping and changing, her hair fair, like his mother's. "Have you any idea what you've done?" her lips breathed, clouding metal.

"No," he said quietly, turning, moving along the counters. "I haven't. Tell me."

She shook her head sadly. "Left us all in our pain. In the

Waste Land. Only you can heal us. Come back," she whispered. "Come home. That's the quest, Cal."

Cal banged into a stand of saucepans; they clattered into a rolling, crashing confusion and the girl's reflection tumbled with them and in the clattering din she looked out at him with twenty covert glances. "Because you did see, didn't you?"

"That place," he said urgently. "Was it real? I didn't just dream it all, did I?"

"You tell me," she said from over his shoulder. "And do you know the pain he's in? That we're all in?"

There were footsteps on the stairs. Cal picked a saucepan up, bewildered. "Back where? It isn't home. It's a ruin."

"It is now." Close behind him, his arms full of aluminum, he felt her push something in his pocket. "Use the sword," she whispered. Though her voice was his.

Lights flickered on. A voice said, "Can I help you, sir?"

In the sudden stark light Cal saw the basement was empty. A man in a white shirt and blue tie was standing on the bottom stair looking at him quizzically.

"Oh, no, sorry. Thanks." He put the pans down quickly. "I just bumped into these," he said quickly. "It was very dark down here."

"Yes. Someone seems to have switched the light off." The man's voice was oddly acid; now they thought he was a shoplifter, Cal thought bitterly, and that it was saucepans he was after. Saucepans!

The man moved to the cash register. "So you aren't interested in buying anything?"

"No," he said firmly, and walked to the stairs.

"Er . . ." The man held out a hand. "Even the CD? I can take care of that here." His grin was spiteful.

"CD?" Cal was blank.

"In your pocket. *Sir.*"

Cal felt for it. It stuck out, still warm from her touch. He pulled it out, not even looking at it, but at the sales assistant, his smile rigid and grim, his heart hammering. "Oh yes," he said tightly. "I'd forgotten about that."

The assistant took it from him. There were hot smudges from his fingers on the cellophane wrapping; the man saw them and smiled coldly. "Happens all the time," he said. He ran the bar code over and took out a plastic bag. "Sixteen fifty."

Cal heard it and managed not to flinch. Elaborately careless, he took out the money and paid it over, only glad he had that much. The man gave him fifty pence change. Silent, Cal turned and stalked up the stairs. He didn't draw a breath till he was out of the store, and then he marched down the steep street without turning or looking right or left, fury burning in him, and humiliation and dismay. Sixteen fifty! Why couldn't he just have said he'd made a mistake, laughed it off! They couldn't have arrested him. That was only when you left the store. Like the time his mother had . . . forgotten about the lager. His ears hot, he stopped and stared sightlessly in a window, taking a deep breath.

The girl had been there. The Grail girl. She must have been.

After a moment he took the plastic bag from his pocket and tipped the CD out, staring at it. It was called *Parsifal*, and it was all in German. And it looked like opera.

Opera!

✠ Seven ✠

*Perceval goeth toward the Deep Forest, that is full broad
and long and evil seeming.*

High History of the Holy Grail

"I can give you a lift home if you hang on till about six."
Trevor had put his head around the office door.

Cal looked up from the pink forms. "Oh," he said.
"Thanks." Then, "What's the earliest I can finish?"

His uncle smiled wryly. "Five. Just because you're the
boss's nephew . . ."

"I'll go then, if you don't mind. I can walk."

Trevor shook his head. "Can't stand the pace, eh? Have
you had a good day?"

"Fine." He didn't know what else to say. When his
uncle had gone and the door was safely shut, he tidied
the mass of forms on the desk into neat piles and
dropped the calculator into the drawer with a sigh. He'd

guessed it might be boring. But this was mind-numbing.

Opposite, Phyllis's vacant computer station blinked strange images over its screen. Phyllis was his uncle's PA, but she was well over fifty and as dry as a stick. She didn't approve of him, he knew. Probably thought he was well-off and spoiled rotten, the boss's nephew getting a job he wasn't qualified for and couldn't do. She certainly wasn't making things easy.

He looked up at the clock. Four-thirty. Thank God for that. It was his fourth day at work, and it had seemed endless. They'd been in the office at eight, because Trevor always liked to be first in, and by ten Cal had been bored rigid. They were giving him the dullest work—start with the basics, Trevor had said, learn the business from the bottom up. He was hardly doing that. Making tea. Opening the post. And they wouldn't even give him a computer yet. All he had done this afternoon was check addresses, postcodes, and put incomprehensible numbers into boxes on pink forms. The trouble was, he knew absolutely nothing about accountancy, tax returns, VAT, all that. Maybe Phyllis was right. Maybe he shouldn't have gotten the job.

He stood up and stretched, yawning. Well, boring or not, it paid real money. And he'd get a day a week in college. He'd learn. Give him five years and he'd be a partner. Ten, and he'd have a chain of offices all of his own, and a flashy car and holidays abroad.

Out of the window, just over the roofs of the next building, he could see a corner of the castle, a dark stone turret. It stopped his thoughts, made him restless, as it had all day, every time he had lifted his eyes from the papers. Probably because of the sword.

Getting it here had been a real pain. He'd wrapped it in a spare T-shirt and then in a plastic bag, and had slipped it into the back of the car when Trevor was giving his impeccable suit a final brush. It would have been just too hard to explain.

Yesterday, he'd found an antique dealer's, in a small alley of tourist shops down by the castle. If he was quick, he could get down there before they closed and sell the thing and be rid of it for good.

He bent and opened the bottom drawer of the desk and looked at the bundle. For a moment he thought of Bron, that bitter agony of disappointment, that pain. Bron had been real. So had the girl. And the cup, the Grail, as she called it. Maybe . . .

The door opened; Phyllis came in and raised an eyebrow. "Packing up?" she asked drily, her sharp eyes going straight to the clock. And quite suddenly Cal couldn't stand the office another minute; the stale room, the stink of the photocopier, the clattering of printers. He picked up the bundle quickly. "Feel a bit queasy. Thought I'd finish early and get some air."

"If that's all right with your uncle," she said so sourly he could almost hear the acid. Dragon, he thought. As soon as he was gone she'd go hissing to Trevor but that could wait. He grabbed his coat from the peg and swung past her. "See you next week," he said to the closed door. He walked fast through the outer office, said good night to the glamorous typist who winked at him, and thundered down the stairs into the street, pulling his coat on and dragging in deep breaths of icy air. Freedom! Thank God.

It was getting dark, the streetlights were coming on, the gleam of lit windows spilling over the pavements. His breath made clouds; he pulled his gloves on and walked quickly, sword under arm, the cold air shocking him back into alertness, his face stinging with the coming night frost.

The quickest way down into town was through Castle Dell. He crossed the road, and the streetlights reddened, dull scarlet glimmers high in the misty darkness. The side street was quiet, with few cars. He followed the railings as far as the gate, and turned into the foggy darkness of the Dell. It sloped deeply into the old dry moat of the castle. On his left were trees, black against the purple twilight, and the concrete path ran down into mist, the lamps smaller here and spread out, their islands of light faint and drifting.

His footsteps were loud; he tried to walk more softly. In daylight this was a busy path, full of dog walkers and small kids out with their mothers, but now in the closing winter night it was lonely and strange and as he went deeper the moat rose around him, crowded with tangled trees and brambles, and behind them, ominously high from down here, the sheer, ruthless bastions of the castle wall.

He stopped, breathing hard. The night smelled of smoke. It was bitterly cold. In front of him the path was black. If there was another lamp the fog had swallowed it. And it seemed to him, with a shiver of fear, that he had done it again, walked straight out of the normal world into some other that was always there waiting for him, in his mind, at twilight, on borders and boundaries, shadowy crossroads. And if he went on, if he walked down there, it would change his whole life, if he didn't turn back right now, back to the lit streets, the office, Trevor's lift in the warm car.

The sword felt awkward, prodding him urgently; he shifted its weight, and looked behind. The frosty halo of the last lamp lit the bark of a tree; far off, down in the town, cars hummed over the bridge. Here, only the breeze moved. He walked on. At once it was colder, as if the sun never got this deep. Spiny branches crowded the path, furred with frost. Gravel crunched underfoot; he pulled the scarf over his face, ducking under twigs. As if he had traveled into some forest, because the path was not like this in the daytime.

Something straight loomed up on his right: a lamppost, dark. Broken glass snapped under his shoes; he moved the pieces with his foot, thoughtfully. And hanging on the branch of a bush was a whole dustbin lid, right in the path. He stopped. The lid was tied, and it swung. As he tried to duck under it the sword struck it hard; there was a great looming clatter. And as if in answer the voice came from behind him. It said, "The mobile phone. And the wallet. Quick!"

Cal turned fast. The man was hard to see, a black shadow. Hefty.

"What?"

"You heard." The man moved in, threatening. "I want the phone and money. Now! And you won't get hurt."

Cal scowled. "I haven't got a mobile phone." Stupidly, he felt annoyed at having to say that.

"Oh yeah. A suit like you." A soft click came out of the dark. Flick knife. Instantly Cal stepped back. He'd been in plenty of fights in Sutton Street. He knew he should run, but it was too dark. And the heavy sword was jabbing at him. *The sword.*

The shadow was close. Cal whipped the bag and wrapping away and held the sword out, slashed wide with it, like they did in the films. It made an icy, whipping slice through the air. A relishing delight. "Right," he muttered. "Come on then." He should never have said that. He had no idea what made him.

Fog drifted. High at his back the castle loomed, its narrow black arrow slits, sheer battlements.

The mugger had flinched back. Now he whistled, sharp, two notes. "You've got a sodding death wish," he whispered.

There were more of them. Cal tried to count, without

looking. Three? Four? He was a fool. For a second he wanted to raise his hand and say, "All right. I've got six quid. It's yours," but it was too late for that. They wanted him now. His blood on the path. And the sword was heavy.

The first one attacked. He came in hard. Cal slashed and yelled and jumped back, into bushes that snagged him, into another shadow that grabbed his arm. The blow was in his stomach; it winded him but he had squirmed sideways and kept hold of the sword, and now he went wild, kicking out, slashing hard with the weapon, screaming and swearing into something that gasped and gave way, the whole sunken forest a racket of battle. They had him pinned; he was dragged down. Something stung his arm; stickiness made the sword slippery. He struggled, yelling again, but the sword was so heavy; a foot slammed into his chest, pain bursting like a star, and for a heartbeat the night went sick and silent.

Then uproar crashed back. More voices. A great deep yell. Bedlam. He was down; they were kicking him and he rolled and scrabbled and knew this was it; he was finished, he was dead, and all at once they were gone. *Gone?*

Cal dragged himself to his knees. The new silence was huge and cold. It had a great hairy hand that gripped his arm and it said, "He's alive, at least."

He groaned, felt sick.

"That's it," the voice said cheerfully. "Take it easy." It turned away. "He's not too bad. A bit shaken up."

Something was dabbing his face; he grabbed it and it was a dirty handkerchief, so he took it and wiped his own blood with it, and realized he was on his hands and knees on the frosty concrete, broken glass stabbing his palms. Torchlight flickered over him.

"Talk to me, mate." A gruff presence hauled him up. "Did they cut you?"

He had no breath, could barely manage, "I don't know." Bruises seemed to be throbbing out all over his body. Foolishly his legs had gone weak; he almost crumpled.

"Take your time," the stranger said, holding him. Then he looked into the darkness. "Shadow? Did they get it?"

"No." A girl's voice; she came out of the night and crouched beside them, all in black, her hair long and straight and inky. "They didn't."

It was the sword she was holding, reverently in both hands, on the palms of her black, fingerless gloves. As she examined it in the torchlight it gleamed, the silver ripples on its blade beautiful, the tiny red jewels eyes of fire.

She looked up at Cal wonderingly, and he saw there was a cobweb tattooed over half her face. "Where in the world did you get this?" she whispered.

✢ Eight ✢

*Men of the Island of Britain most courteous to guests
and strangers: Gwalchmai, son of Gwyar . . .*

Trioedd Ynys Prydein

"What'll it be? I've got a few cans."

Cal lowered himself painfully into the chair. His whole
body ached. "I don't drink," he muttered.

"He needs hot sweet tea." The girl ducked under the curtain that screened the door of the van and put the sword carefully on the table. "Don't you . . . ?" She left a space for his
name so he said, "Cal," and shrugged, numb. "Whatever."
Now it was over he couldn't stop shaking.

The man nodded, putting the kettle on. "No problem."
He was older than the girl; muscular, his hair razored short.
Even in this cold he wore only a check shirt, tight over his
shoulders, and jeans. The girl sat opposite. "He's the Hawk.
You can call me Shadow."

Cal was looking at his hands, and his trousers. Blood, mud, everywhere. "God what a mess," he mumbled.

"Did they get anything?"

"Nothing to get."

She had a clean cloth; she squeezed water out of it and gave it to him, then went to a cluttered cupboard on the wall and rummaged there, coming back with a small tube of ointment. "Let's have a look at you."

Before he could object she had his coat off; he pulled his shirt up gingerly. The cut was shallow under his ribs, beaded with blood, but it had slashed right through shirt and jacket. He felt suddenly very sick. "God," he whispered.

"Mmm. A bit deeper and it doesn't bear thinking about." She cleaned it quickly, and he hissed with the sting, looking around at the inside of the van, trying to get his mind clear, to get the terror out that had come now, too late. The van was warm and stuffy. It smelled of incense and dirty socks and bananas. Some sort of camp stove sizzled in one corner, and it was incredibly untidy. Every surface was draped and swathed with colorful fabrics, wall hangings and curtains, subtle rich velvets of purple and maroon embroidered with gold, beaded with tiny crystals. Sunflowers were painted on the table, almost obliterated now with brown rings from the bottoms of mugs, and down one window a great sun rose in stained glass, glowing with haloes of brilliant color. Tasteful it was not, he thought wryly. Next to it, hanging on the wall, were swords. Real swords. Cal flinched.

"Sorry," the girl said absently.

A shield was propped by the door. A pentangle was painted on it. A stack of spears, or lances. A helmet. He gave a quick glance at the big man pouring tea, then at the dog-eared books on the yellow shelf. *Armor of the Fifteenth Century. The Sword in Medieval Combat. Sir Gawayne and the Grene Knight.* What sort of madhouse had he stumbled into this time? The mess annoyed him, reminded him of the flat. He had a desperate desire to start cleaning it all up.

"Right." The girl looked up, the tattoo on her face a lace-work in the lamplight. "That doesn't look too bad. What else?" He opened his sticky, slashed palms.

"Yuck. Keep still, it'll hurt." Her long glossy hair fell forward as she worked. He saw she wore only black; filmy layers of it, skirt over skirt over trousers, and heavy men's boots.

"Tea." Hawk came and put it down. He sat on the cluttered sofa, pushing off a small cat, put his feet up, and watched. "You were lucky there, laddie. If we hadn't come along . . ."

"Yes. Thanks." Cal felt annoyance welling up. "If he'd been on his own I could have handled him."

"Maybe. You were up for it. But not with that technique."

"What?"

"Swordplay. You were wide open, slashing like that. If they'd had any sense one would have been in under your arm."

"Hawk," the girl said quietly.

He stopped, then raised his eyebrows. "Just saying, lady."

"Then stop saying."

The big man leaned back. "Well, I knocked a couple of their heads together for you. And she marked one on the face, didn't you?"

Shadow smiled coyly. "Get him something to eat." She dropped the bloodstained cloth into the dish and looked at Cal's hands carefully. "I'll bandage them up, if you like." He frowned, thinking instantly of Trevor. If Trevor thought he'd been in some fight . . . "Have you got any Band-Aids?" he asked quickly. "It's just, they wouldn't show so much."

She gave him a glance. Then she said, "I'll see if I can find any."

Hawk came back and put some plates on the table; there was a new, garlicky smell in the warm air. "Microwave," he explained. "Bit high-tech, I know, but I can run it off the solar panel. My brother fixed it up." He sat. "Unless you want to go to the hospital."

Cal tried to pick up the hot cup. "I hate hospitals."

"Might need a stitch in that side."

"No."

"Police then?"

Cal shrugged, unbearably weary. "I'd rather not." It was Trevor he kept thinking of. This wouldn't impress him. And behind it all, thin as an icy thread, the terror of being sent back home.

They sat in silence until Shadow came back and made him open his palms; she pressed the Band-Aids on gently, but it still hurt, and he bit his lip.

"That's the best I can do."

"Thanks." The tea was hot, but it helped. He felt very strange; weak and trembly. He hadn't felt scared out there, but now it was all coming over him in waves. Maybe the girl noticed. She said, "Who were they?"

"Muggers. Wanted money."

"Black Knights," Hawk said, rubbing the cat. "Or this century's version. You won't see them again. We'll walk you home later. You live close?"

"Otter's Brook." He was intensely proud, for a second. Then the name seemed shallow and ridiculous.

Hawk whistled. "Nice. Expensive. So, now, I'm desperate to know: What's a nice suburban lad in a suit doing with a sword in Castle Dell?"

Cal felt hot. The microwave pinged, and the big man groaned and got up to see to it. Shadow said quickly, "He could teach you how to use the sword properly." She reached out and touched its edge. "It deserves someone who knows what they're doing."

Cal sipped the tea. "I'm selling it."

They both stared at him, astonished. Hawk left the food and came back fast. "What? You can't!"

"Make me an offer."

"Do you know what that weapon is?"

"A pain in the neck."

"Cal, this is serious." Hawk picked the sword up, carefully as the girl had done, weighing it in both hands. Then he took the corded grip firmly and raised the blade upright so that it shone in the bright room. "This is a very powerful weapon. Magical. We should take it to the Company and let them see it. Arthur will know what to do. You can't sell it, it's not that sort of possession."

Cal glared at him. "It started that fight," he said.

Hawk didn't flinch. "I can well believe it. I've come across such weapons before. They have their own will. How did you get it?"

Miserable, Cal shrugged. "A man gave it to me."

Hawk glanced at Shadow. "Go on," she said. And quite suddenly Cal knew that he wanted to tell them, and that he was hungry, as if he hadn't eaten for days. "Dish that stuff up. And I will."

"Won't they be expecting you at home?"

Cal almost laughed. He had discovered that Trevor always ate out. Cal had spent every evening on his own so far, and though he was used to that, he didn't want it tonight, he realized.

"No." He put the empty cup down. "Deal?"

Hawk wrapped the sword. "Deal."

To his own amazement Cal enjoyed all of it. The spicy food, the chipped plates, the warm, cluttered, comfortable room; after a while all of them stopped hurting him. Hawk lay on the sofa with his feet up and plate balanced on his chest, and Shadow sat cross-legged on the floor and fed the cat tidbits. They drank beer out of cans, and he told them. About the train, and the walk in the dark, and about Corbenic. It was strange; he didn't know them, but he trusted them. He told them about Bron, the man's tormented unhappiness, and about the great banquet. And then he told them about the Grail.

At first Hawk chipped in, asking questions, but when Cal described the procession, the power of the shining cup, the spear that bled on the floor, he was silent. Except that in the curved reflection of the shield, Cal saw him glance at Shadow, and her shake of the head. He stopped, suspicious. "Have you heard this story before? From someone else?" He sat up. "Do you know about this place?"

Shadow looked uneasy. "We've heard of it. Tell us the end. What happened after?"

Cal put the plate down and picked at his sore hands. Then he said, "Nothing."

"Nothing?"

"Bron . . . he seemed to want me to do something. Ask him something."

"And you didn't?"

"No," he whispered. The cat got up and wandered out, beyond the bright hangings. "I said I hadn't seen anything."

The van was silent. Only the stove hissed, and the wind outside, over the castle walls. Suddenly, Cal looked up. "I know, I lied. It was . . . I just couldn't understand what was going on. I thought it was . . . the drink. And in the morning, it was gone. As if it was all a dream." He couldn't explain. Not about his mother and her voices. Not about home.

Shadow said, "Cal, listen to me. Have you tried to get back to this place?"

"Why should I?"

She looked at Hawk. "Tell him."

The big man was sitting up now, his great arms folded over his chest. He looked grave. "There was once a King . . ." he said.

"I don't want some fairy tale!" Cal almost stood, but Hawk reached over and shoved him down, hard.

"You're not getting one. This man was the ruler over a great country. In his castle were secrets, terrible secrets. He was the guardian of the Grail, a cup that held great mysteries, some say a cauldron, or the chalice of the Last Supper. Also the Lance, the Sword, the Stone; ancient Hallows. The Grail came to this island centuries ago, and while the King was whole the land was at peace. But these things are dangerous, they give pain as well as joy. It happened that the King was wounded by a blow from the Lance itself, and completely crippled, and his pain . . . it infected all the land. The country became a waste land. Desolate. Wintry. The people's hearts became hard."

"Don't tell me," Cal sneered. "Murders and muggings and sink estates. Pollution, pornography. Drugs. Right?"

"In one." Hawk wouldn't let him go; the man's hand was heavy, a hard grip. "It might not be like that in Otter's Brook, my son, but not everyone's as privileged as you. And the King moaned and wept but he couldn't be cured, he can never be cured, until someone comes, someone they all wait for."

"And he spends his time fishing, and they call him the Fisher King?" Cal twisted away. "Get real. I thought you were different but you're not. You're just winding me up." It was all wrong. They didn't believe him. He should never have told them. And Bron's words were whispering in his ear. *You ask me. That's all you need to do. Ask me about what you saw.*

Shadow knelt up and put her drink down; her fingernails were black too, with delicate crystals stuck on her nails. "We're not. Listen to him."

"It's just a story! Fine! I suppose if I'd asked Bron about the Grail he'd have been cured, would he? On the spot? He'd have jumped up and gone dancing? And I'd have come back and found us all living in country cottages with roses growing round the door? No one in the jails or sleeping rough or ill and my mother . . ." He stopped instantly, confused, cursing himself. Then he shoved Hawk's hand away and looked around for his coat.

"It's a story, yes," Shadow said urgently, "but stories mean things. You must have dreamed it for a reason . . ."

"Sure." He pulled his coat on, ignoring her, ignoring the stab of pain in his side. "I must be crazy talking to a pair of New Age weirdos. Look at you!" he gestured around angrily. "Look at this place!"

Hawk folded his arms. "Cal," he said gently.

Hurt, furious, Cal shoved him aside, pulled the curtain so hard he almost tore it, and fumbled blindly for the door. To his horror hot tears were pricking his eyes. He had to get out. To get away. He stumbled down the steps of the van into the frosty fog and half walked, half ran over the mud.

"Wait!" Shadow's darkness loomed after him. "You've left the sword. Cal!"

"Keep it," he growled, not caring if she heard him or not. "Keep the bloody thing."

He walked fast, unthinking, wiping his face. He didn't care where he went, but in the swirls of fog the streets opened before him, uphill, past the shuttered shops, under the town arch, past the lit fronts of pubs where voices and music and cigarette smoke drifted out through opened windows.

By Otter's Brook the fog was thinner, and he was weary, slower, his side and chest throbbing, and he shivered in the cheap suit. The key was ice cold; he fumbled with it, opened the door, and slid in quickly, leaning with his back against it, breathing deep, harshly, every gasp almost a sob. *Calm down.* He had to calm down.

The room was warm, and spotless. Nothing disturbed it. It smelled of Thérèse's perfume. He kicked his shoes off, ran upstairs and pulled off trousers and shirt frantically, then ran down and stuffed them into the washing machine. It started, a heavy thumping. Then he dressed, put the TV on and went and sat in front of it, watching, not seeing. He only wanted noise. People laughing. People he didn't know, laughing.

There was a note on the table. He had stared at it a long while before he even saw it; then the words jumped out at him, in Trevor's fastidious handwriting. *Your mother rang. Wants you to phone back. Sounds desperate.*

"God," he said aloud. *God.* He couldn't. Not now, not tonight. Tomorrow. Not now.

Suddenly, out of nowhere, he remembered the slashed jacket, and he searched desperately for some matching thread, and found it in one of the orderly kitchen cupboards. He sewed the slash in the jacket carefully, hurriedly, stabbing his thumb, but he couldn't do it fast enough, because even as he finished and bit the thread the phone rang with a jolt that seemed to go right through him. He stared at it, unmoving. It rang. Over and over. Never stopping. Never changing.

"Hang up," he whispered, in agony. "Hang up." But she didn't. The same two notes, insistent, urgent, getting to him, getting inside him till his nerves were so tight his chest ached and he wanted to scream. And then it stopped, halfway through a ring. The silence was shocking. It was only nine o'clock but he had to hide from it; he flicked the TV off and ran upstairs and got into bed and lay there, breathless. He thought he had loved the silence, but it was a threat now; it could be broken. Sweating, he waited, every muscle tense in the bed. The torment lasted ten minutes. Then the phone rang. And rang.

He groped for the Walkman, for anything. The only CD on the bedside table was the opera the girl had shoved in his pocket. Now, hands shaking, sobbing, he tore the frail plastic off and jammed it in, switching on and pulling the earphones on, curling deep under the bedclothes.

The music was loud. It swallowed everything. It blocked out the whole world. It was a great orchestra and choruses of voices, men and women, conflicting and chiming and rising and falling with each other. He didn't know what they sang about, only that it was passionate, it was pure and holy, it could protect him, that while it played he couldn't hear the phone, feel the bruises, didn't have to remember his mother, the guilt, his fear of sliding into mental illness.

Hours later, when Trevor looked in and muttered, "Good night, Cal," he lay still, exhausted, as if asleep, his ears numb. But his heart beat too fast in his chest, like a bird's.

✤ Nine ✤

Listen, little pig
We should hide
from the huntsman of Mordei
lest we be discovered . . .

Oıanau of Merlin

Maybe to punish himself, he had the dream. He was six, and they were on that bus. The one to the seaside, the one he had looked forward to for days, the one where he stood on the seat and looked out of the window at the strange houses, the amazingly green fields, the great mountains.

She had a small flask in her bag and she was always sipping from it, and when she stood up the bus swayed, and she fell down.

"Mam," he had said. "Mam?"

And the woman behind had got up and shouted, "Stop the bus! This woman's sick."

And she had been, all over the floor and the bag and the sandwiches, and he had huddled in the seat and watched as a man helped her off, and she was giggling then, and dropping coins from her purse, and the women all around had been saying words in hard, unforgiving voices, words he had heard before in the playground, outside the school—drunk, drink, drunken, drunkard—cries like the chorus of gulls that had echoed all the hot afternoon on the sand. She had slept curled up in the chair on the beach for hours, burned by the sun, and he had paddled and dug holes and cried and got cold, and then he had asked the man who sold the deckchairs why his mother didn't wake up. That was the first time they had gone to the hospital. And the nurses had given him a bar of chocolate and phoned the police.

He opened his eyes. This wasn't dreaming, it was remembering, and he never allowed himself to do it. It was against his rules. There had to be rules, and he had to keep them.

He sat up. There were voices downstairs; that meant Thérèse had stayed the night, and he was glad, because he liked to talk to her, and she was always laughing. And she was pretty.

He dressed quickly, pleased that his clothes were clean, wishing he had another sweater, because the green one was getting worn. Maybe when his first paycheck came . . . And he'd ring, he thought all at once, halfway down the open-plan stair. He'd ring home, but not yet, because she wouldn't be up yet. Not for hours.

"So he's given you Saturdays off?" Thérèse laughed. She

was making toast in the unused kitchen, the smell of it mingling with coffee and a small bunch of freesias by the sink.

"Only while he's on probation," Trevor said from behind the paper.

Thérèse winked at Cal.

"These are nice." He touched the yellow flowers.

"I bought them. To brighten up the place. Have you noticed, Cal, there are no flowers. No plants. Not even a garden. It would drive me mad."

Cal poured coffee. "Is that why you don't live here?" For a second, he thought he had offended her. Then she smiled brightly and tapped him on the nose. "Mind yours. Your uncle and I have our own places. That's the way it is."

The toaster clunked, and she took the bread out. There were croissants too, he noticed with pleasure, and fresh butter.

Cal wandered into the long room and put his plate on the table; his uncle glanced at him. "In fact I ought to insist you go in this morning. What's this about you sliding off at half four last night?"

"Phyllis," Cal said bitterly.

"Yes. And she was right. It's not on, Cal."

The doorbell rang; Thérèse went, her white shirt loose over tight dark trousers.

Cal chewed the flaky croissant. "It won't happen again. I just felt . . . a bit . . ."

"No, it won't. I wouldn't take it from anyone else and I

won't take it from you." He tipped his head, curious. "And what on earth have you done to your hand?"

Before he could think of an answer, Thérèse was calling from the door, "Cal?" Her voice was coy. "It's for you," she said, and there was a mocking note in it that surprised him. Until he looked over and saw Shadow.

She was standing outside the front door, wearing the same clothes as last night, and she smiled calmly, hands in pockets. "Hi," she said.

"Hi." He was numb with embarrassment; the word came out automatically. She seemed so out of place here. The cobweb on her face was a mystery, her dark scruffy clothes bizarre in the modern, spotless room.

He got up hastily and went over; Thérèse winked and slipped discreetly into the kitchen. He glanced back; Trevor was watching with ill-disguised astonishment over the newspaper.

"What are you doing here?" Cal whispered.

"You're not so hard to find." She scratched her cheek with a black fingernail. "Hawk kept an eye on you last night."

"Followed me!"

"If you like. Because of the sword."

"I told you . . ."

"Come on, Cal. We can't keep it."

"*I don't want it.*" He shot an uneasy look in the mirror. He should ask her in, but her boots were muddy. The thought turned him cold.

"And we thought you might want to see Hawk fight."

"Fight?"

"At the reenactment. You could meet the rest of the Company." She smiled, teasing. "We want you to come."

"What Company?"

"Arthur's. It's a reenactment group."

He hesitated. It was the last thing he wanted. But he had to get her out of here.

"Bring your friend in," Trevor said with vast reluctance.

"Oh, it's okay. We're just going out." Cal ran back and gulped his coffee; then raced upstairs and snatched his coat from the wardrobe, cursing and dashing back to brush his teeth. But when he got back downstairs again Shadow was sitting on the soft leather sofa talking to Thérèse.

Cal fidgeted at the door. "We're going down to the castle."

Trevor managed to take his eyes off Shadow's tattoo long enough to say, "Fine." He looked horrified; made a blank, questioning face. Cal shrugged, hot.

"Enjoy yourselves!" From the doorstep Thérèse waved them off. Cal knew as soon as she went back in she'd collapse in fits of giggles and Trevor would fling the paper down and say, "Who the hell was THAT?"

He stalked down the sloping drive, furious with himself and furious with Shadow for coming. She didn't seem to notice. Instead she walked behind him slowly and said, "Is your mother French?"

94

"*What?*"

"She sounds it."

Amazed, he realized she was talking about Thérèse. He opened his mouth to tell her Thérèse was his uncle's girlfriend. Instead he said, "Yes." That's how easy it was. One word. And you could create a whole new world. She probably thought Trevor was his father. He had never had a father. In an instant a vivid string of imaginings had come and gone in his mind; him at six with Thérèse in the park, his birthday parties, Christmas, skiing, summer holidays at their place in France, Trevor and Thérèse proud at parents' evenings. He stopped, and let her catch up. Finally he said, "God knows what they think."

"Let them." She shrugged. "Hawk sent me. He says the sword is too important, and he knows about things like that. It's his job."

"What is?"

"Reenacting battles. Pretending to be King Arthur's Knights."

"Fighting!" Cal was scathing. "Dressing up like some relic from the Crusades. It's sad."

She grinned at him. "It's fun. Highly educational for the kids. Lighten up, Cal." Suddenly serious, she looked at him sideways. "We both think you're in trouble."

They were walking under the town arch. It was hollow, dripping, a medieval gateway with trucks scraping under it. He said, awkward, "I'm sorry about last night. I get . . . uptight."

"You'd had a shock."

"I thought he was making fun of me."

Shadow stepped aside for a woman with a stroller. Then she said, "Hawk believes you. That you were really there."

"What about you?" he asked bitterly. She didn't answer. Instead she pointed. "There's the one you need to talk to."

Across the street, outside Woolworth's, a man was selling the *Big Issue*. He was incredibly scruffy, his long coat a sort of patchwork, his hair tangled, but he was quick and agile, his words holding passersby, his long hands supple as he talked till they dragged out a few grudging coins. Behind him on the pavement, a lanky brown dog lay curled.

"Who's he?"

"The Hermit." Shadow caught his elbow. "Come on." She crossed the road, pulling him with her. Appalled, he said, "Great."

The man stank. Cal could smell him already, an unwashed stench mixed with beer and some woody earthiness like soil in rain. His eyes were dark as Bron's but lit with a wildness that made Cal wary; it reminded him of his mother at her worst times. When the man saw them he gripped Shadow's shoulders; his hands were bony and the nails had been bitten to the quick. "So it's you, Webbed One."

"It's me, master. I've brought someone to meet you." She turned, and Cal knew she was enjoying his distaste. "This is Cal."

The man looked at him hard. His face was thin, scabbed, stubbled with a scraggy beard, his hair a tangle over the crazy eyes. He held out his hand and, infinitely disgusted, Cal took it. "Not your real name." The grin was wolf-sharp; all at once the Hermit's tough grip felt like the paw of some beast.

Cal snatched his hand away. "It's the name I like."

"We're none of us what we seem." The man gave a sideways nod at Shadow. "She hides in darkness. You in daylight."

Cal was rubbing the grease from his fingers. "What about you?"

"I hide in time. My name is Merlin."

Behind them, the dog yawned. Instantly the man turned; a sudden frenzy of anger transformed him. "And there's her!" He spat. "My death. Always watching. Waiting at my heels." He gave a vicious lunge toward the dog, stamping at it. "Bitch! Get away!" It took not the slightest notice, but lay down and looked at them with soft eyes.

Cal was backing off. He was on the point of turning and going, anywhere, but Shadow caught his sleeve and said, "We're going to watch the Hawk."

"Not only you. The others are all there. All of Arthur's Company." The Hermit was eyeing Cal; now he leaned close, the smell pungent. "But you need to make a phone call first," he whispered. "And she won't be where you expect her." A scruffy magazine was pushed into Cal's hands. "Take this."

Cal swallowed. "Thanks. Very much. We have to go now."

He threw Shadow a desperate glance; was already moving off. What if someone saw him? What if *Trevor* saw him!

The Hermit smiled a wolfish smile. "We'll speak again. But not yet, Shadow."

She nodded. "If you say so, master."

"God!" Cal said, safely down the street. "You know some weird people!"

"Yes. I know you." She smiled secretly. "But he was right about your name, wasn't he?"

"Maybe." They had come to a phone box; Cal almost managed to walk past it. Then he stopped. "I don't know how he guessed, but he was right about the phone call too. You go on. I'll catch you up."

"I'll wait," she said sweetly, sitting on the curb.

Cal squeezed in and picked up the receiver. He dialed his home number. At the other end the phone rang, and kept ringing. At first he felt relief, then guilt. And fear. Where was she? What was going on? He couldn't put the receiver down. He seemed frozen there, listening to the ringing in the empty house. And then, as he scratched his face with the rolled-up magazine in his hand, he saw what he was holding wasn't the *Big Issue* at all, but a stiff parchment of pages, empty except for the number that had been scrawled on the front page. A phone number. A Bangor number. Slowly, he put the handset down, and stared at the number. *She won't be where you expect her.*

A truck roared past. Shadow called and waved to someone driving it.

Cal picked up the phone again, and dialed. It was crazy. But. A voice answered, almost immediately. "Hello?" A man. Cal gripped the phone tight. Panic started to rise; a pain on his chest.

"I want . . . Could I speak to Annie Davies? Is she there?" He was sweating. Praying. This couldn't be. But the man said, "Hang on. I'll get her."

✱ Ten ✱

*Ladies and damsels climbed into towers and peered through the
wall battlements, thronging at windows to see the knights joust.*

Didot-Perceval

He had always loathed the men. Over the years there had
been many, and four who'd stayed around for a few months
each, one almost a year. Cal had been sullen, barely able to
speak to them, even Aled, who'd been so free-handed with his
money and had given him that denim jacket when he was
thirteen. But it had been cheap and tacky and he'd sold it.
They'd taken her out, and she'd laughed and seemed happy;
sometimes he'd let himself almost think one of them might
make a difference. But the voices had always come back, and
the gin to drown them out. And when the men had gone she
was worse. Now, maybe, there was another one. He waited,
watching Shadow through the glass door, feeding a pigeon
crumbs from her pockets.

Breathy sounds. A scuffle. Then, "Cal? Is that you?"

"Mam? Where are you?"

She laughed. It wasn't the usual giggle. *She was sober.* A huge relief washed over him; his very bruises seemed to stop aching.

"I'm at Rhian's."

"Who's Rhian?"

"She's my new outworker. From the hospital. We went to a group session last night and it was late so I stayed over." She laughed again, a light sound. "What did you think? New boyfriend?"

He shrugged. "Sort of." He couldn't remember the last time she had sounded like this.

"I rang you last night but you must have been out. I wanted to tell you how I feel so good, Cal! These people—Dr. Lewis got me onto the program—they're really helping me. I'm going to sort things out, Cal, I really am this time."

Looking out up the crowded street he said, "That's great, Mam."

"You don't think I can do it, do you?"

"Of course I do. If you get the help. It's just . . ." He stopped, hating himself, but she hadn't even been listening.

"I've had my hair done, Cal. Rhian came with me. You should see the little blond highlights! And this new medication, it's so good! I can sleep, and there are no voices anymore; no one talking to me all the time."

He let her go on; it spilled out of her and he listened to it, thinking how empty the house must be for her, without him. She'd cleaned and hoovered, she said, and done the washing. "And tomorrow the whole group's going out for a meal. Nice people they are. And no wine." Her voice was low, close to the receiver. "I'm right off that, Cal."

"Great!" he said. "I'm really proud of you." Thinking of the last time she'd said that, of the day he'd come home deliriously pleased with his exam results and found the bottles under the sink. How he had taken them into the street and smashed them, one by one, green glass and blue and white, sobbing in fury, and the shards had cut him. How she'd screamed and screamed. How the neighbors had come out.

Shadow was watching. She looked impatient. "Come on!" she mouthed against the glass.

He nodded, turned away. "Listen, Mam, I'm glad things are okay. I've got to go now. My friends are waiting."

"Cal," she said, her voice choked, "I know I drove you away."

His heart thumped. "It wasn't like that."

"Yes, it was. I don't blame you."

"No . . ."

"And when I get straight it'll be different. You'll be proud to come home. Rhian says I can do it, and I will."

He smiled, wan. "I've got to go. . . ."

"But you will come home next weekend, won't you? You can see my new hair."

"Okay." He was lying, he knew he was, but he was help-
less. "Next Saturday. Bye, Mam. The money's running out."

"I love you, Cal," she said quickly. Then the insistent bleep
nagged the silence and he put the receiver down and the coins
clunked into the box. Wearily, he put the other pound back
into his pocket and pushed the heavy door wide.

"You were a time!" Shadow looked at him closely. "Everything all right? Not bad news?"

"No. Not bad at all." The sun shone in his eyes; suddenly
he felt it was true, and that surge of happiness came back, the
same pride he had felt when he'd first walked out of Otter's
Brook. "Come on," he said. "Let's go and see this fight."

The castle was hung with flags. As Cal ran after Shadow
down the long, sloping path he saw that this morning the
Dell was full of tents and vans; a sudden garish encampment
that had mushroomed up in the sun, peopled by men in
chainmail and bits of clanky plate armor and jeans, by a
smith banging horseshoes on a vast anvil, by women in long
dresses and braided hair cooking messes of stew in precarious
cauldrons. There were kids everywhere, pinned and laced
into a patchwork of homemade historical costumes, some
with their faces painted with incongruous tigers or Welsh
dragons. The smoke of fires hung low, the smell of sizzling
meat and onions eye-wateringly strong from the hot dog van
at the edge of the car park, and somewhere someone was

playing a harp, the fine twang almost drowned out by the eleven o'clock news thundering from a radio hung on a stack of spiked halberds.

"What is all this?"

Shadow grinned. "A meeting of reenacters. I told you."

"And they're going to fight each other? All of them?"

She picked her way past a pile of steaming horse manure. "Watch your step. No, not like a battle. Hawk says they have those, but this is more like . . . a tournament. For Advent."

"Advent?"

"Arthur called it. He always likes to celebrate the old feast days. Says he won't sit down to eat till something really way-out has happened."

But Cal had stopped by a stall selling weapons, and she went back for him slowly. Swords of every period and variety hung there: rapiers, épées, foils, claymores, falchions; short Roman stabbing blades, huge unwieldable medieval broadswords. He stared at the prices almost in dismay. "These things cost a fortune."

"Good replicas always do." Shadow tapped a hanging dagger; it clinked against the others in the row. Then she said, "None of them are as special as your sword. The Company are looking after it. They'll know what to do."

A trumpet rang out in the castle, and a loudspeaker rumbled blurred words inside the walls. Shadow grabbed his arm. "Come on! We'll miss him!" She pushed through a crowd of visitors packing the gloomy tunnel of the gatehouse and out into a vast grassy courtyard lined with spectators kept back by a white rope on pegs hammered into the mud. On all four sides the walls of the castle rose, lined with people. Some families had picnic rugs or folding chairs; from crumbling windows in Marten's tower excited kids watched, gripped firmly by the shoulders, and along the battlements a whole court smoked and catcalled and ate, a bizarre confusion of fashions and epochs. Most were in medieval dress, but there were a few Roman legionnaires, a crusader knight, and a whole gang of Roundheads, leaning nonchalantly on huge pikes. High on the tower top sat a noisy row of Vikings, their legs through the safety rails, drinking from cans passed from hand to hand. An empty can was tossed down and just missed Cal, who glared up. The Vikings jeered.

"Here," Shadow said.

The trumpets brayed again, loud and close. She ran up a flight of stone steps built against the curtain wall, and Cal followed. The steps were steep and irregular; at the top he pushed among the spectators until he could find a space, and glancing behind him he saw that they were high on the castle's brink, and far below was the Dell's green moat, and beyond that the town, and the estuary, and the white and silver spans of the Severn bridges.

"Here he comes!" She sounded proud, full of laughter.

Cal turned, and stared. A gaudy procession of armed men,

horses, banners. And on the first horse, bareheaded in a chainmail hauberk and a surcoat blazing with the image of a golden sun, was the Hawk. Shadow yelled at him and he saw them, waving up and blowing kisses, and Cal saw he wore a heavy sword and two boys marched behind him with a plumed helmet and a lance. "He's going to *joust*! He must be crazy!"

Shadow smiled a secret smile. "He's good at it. You watch."

The other knight wore blue, pale blue, and his helmet was crested with a leaping cat; Cal wondered at how heavy it must be. In the cleared center of the tiltyard a long space had a frail barrier down the center; marshals with white batons conferred there, calling complex instructions, gesturing the crowd back. The two knights, one at each end, were handed up their lances, heavy, unmaneuverable things, but Hawk tucked his up expertly and brought the horse around, its yellow caparison already mudflecked, its eyes in the wide holes of the golden cloth white and tense. He made a strange flamboyant salute, but not to them; to a group of people on the tower, a man in a tweed suit, and a tall man behind him, and a woman with long blond hair.

"Who are they?"

"Quiet! This is it."

The horses backed, snorting. Drums were rolling, an ominous thunder. In the hushed crowd a baby cried. At the very

center of the lists, the marshal's baton came down. The cro
roared. The horses began to run, straight at each other; t
lances swiveled down. There was a terrifying second of expe
tation, then the blue knight's lance sliced over Hawk's shoul
der and they were past each other, and Hawk was at the far
end, wheeling around. Before Cal could speak they came
again, the thunder of the hooves vibrating deep in the turf
and the stones, the lances deadly and long, and even as he saw
with a shock of fear that there was no padding, that they were
real, Hawk's lance struck the round shield of the blue knight
with a crack, splintering, flinging the man down and off with
a sickening thud on the grass. The crowd went mad, screaming their praise.

"This is crazy! He might be hurt!" Cal's yell was lost, but
Shadow just shook her head and pointed. The blue knight
was on his feet.

Still crazy, Cal thought. But the excitement was burning in
him, too, he knew that as he watched Hawk leap down and
hand his horse to a boy who ran out for it and then draw his
sword.

The blue knight flung off his helmet. He had a dark
tanned face; he winked at Hawk. Then he attacked.

"Is this a setup?" Cal had Shadow by the shoulder.

"What?"

"Like a stage fight!" He had to shout in her ear. "Or is
it real?"

She looked at him then, strangely, and her answer was so low he barely heard it. "They'll never say."

The swords rang and clashed. He knew nothing of this but it stirred him; he could see how the attacks were swept in, feinted, covered; how the parries worked to block and protect the body, that there were ways of balancing and using the other's weight and force against him, that it was a whole science, a beautiful, deadly dance. Hawk slashed; the crowd gasped as the blue knight ducked barely in time, then rushed in, cutting right and left into the rock-steady parries, twisting, swinging swiftly around to avoid a vertical slice of the hissing blade.

Shadow was yelling, jumping up and down, and so was he, he realized, shouting, "Hawk! Come on!" and other useless nonsense, and it was back, something of that crazy desperate longing that he had felt before the Grail, that hunger, that loss of himself. "Hawk!" he screamed, and the golden knight turned with a great roar and smashed his opponent's sword aside so that it flew and skidded over the muddy grass.

Everyone flung their arms up and cheered.

And the blue knight knelt gasping, breathless, and laughed, and Hawk leaned on his sword and laughed with him, sweat dripping from his chin.

And in that instant, a bird plummeted out of the sky. A sudden, violent shock, it screamed down straight into Cal's face; he flung an arm up, caught a fluttering screech of

hooked beak, a cold eye, felt the rake of talons. Then he was down, people around him scattering and yelling, Shadow dragging him and the bird diving at him again, a demented, terrifying slash so that he beat at it and flung his arms over his head, a hot scratch searing down his face.

"Cal! It's gone. Are you all right?"

Carefully, he uncurled. "What the hell was it?" he gasped.

"A bird. Some sort of falcon. It seemed to go right for you."

"An osprey." A woman in a fifteenth-century shift pointed up. "There it is."

It had risen, far into the blue, a point of darkness. Three times it screamed around the castle, every eye following it, until it swooped down and down onto the arm of a huge brawny red-haired man outside in the encampment. Cal was hanging so far out over the wall to see, Shadow had to grab him. The falconer looked up, one look. Sour. Then he was gone in the crowd.

"Who was it?" Shadow stared. "Did you know him?"

"That was Leo." Blood ran onto his lip; he could taste it.

"From that . . . from Corbenic?"

"I'm sure it was him."

"Cal!"

He turned. Hawk was down on the grass, pushing through the crowd that was streaming toward the archery butts set out in the upper barbican. When he reached the foot of the wall he stared up, the sweat still gleaming on him. "Are you all right?"

"Fine." Cal mopped the blood up with a tissue. "Great."

The sarcasm was wasted. Hawk just nodded. "The Company want to meet you. Come on."

At the end of the battlements was a small door marked PRIVATE. Ignoring that, Hawk opened it and led them in, and in the sudden dimness Cal saw he was in a tower room, the floor made of planks of wood, an apple-wood fire burning in the great hearth against one wall. He saw the blond-haired woman turn to him, and then, sitting by the fire, the man in the tweed suit, who looked up as they came in. He had a grave face, and for a moment Cal thought he seemed like a university type, a lecturer. And then he thought, No. A soldier.

The man had Cal's sword on his knees. "So," he said, looking hard at Cal, his voice soft. "This weapon was given to you? You must be someone very special." The sword gleamed, its red stones bright in the flame light.

"And you must be Arthur," Cal said.

Arthur stood. "Yes," he said mildly. "So I am. This is Gwen, my wife. And my seneschal, Kai." The tall man. So handsome that Cal hated him on sight. And the long dark coat had to be Armani, at least.

Kai smiled, slightly mocking. "Your face is cut. Why did the bird attack you?"

"My business." He took a step forward and held his hands out. "That's my sword. I want it."

"Do you?" Arthur gestured toward Hawk. "My nephew tells me you want to sell it."

"That was yesterday. Things are better today."

"But what will you do with it?"

"Learn to use it." Cal glanced at Hawk. "I'd like to learn. If you'd teach me."

"We'll all teach you, laddie," Hawk said heartily.

"Indeed," Kai said acidly. "You'll need all of us."

Cal turned to Arthur, who held the sword out in both hands.

"Then take it back, and everything that it means, and be one with us, Cal."

Slowly, Cal reached out and took it, the weight of the metal, warm from the fire, put his fingers around the blade, held it tight.

Arthur smiled. "Welcome to the Company."

Behind him, Kai folded his arms. "Maybe now we can eat," he muttered.

❖ Spear ❖

❖ Eleven ❖

"Go thy way," said she, "to Arthur's court, where are the best of men, and the most generous and bravest."

Peredur

December was already halfway over. The weather had chilled; as he waited on the corner of Otter's Brook, Cal saw that the last few leaves which had clung onto the trees only yesterday were gone now, blown away by the blustery wind. As he watched them their stark bare shapes offended his longing for order—trees were so haphazard; he wanted to straighten them up. Plunging his hands in his pockets he paced the pavement, kicking rotten leaves into the gutter. He didn't know what any of the trees were called. In Sutton Street there had never been any, just the stubborn weeds that sprouted every year from the cracks in the paved yard.

Hawk's van rattled around the corner. Cal picked up the sword in its canvas case and ran over.

"Sorry." Shadow had the door open, breathless. "Couldn't get it to start. We daren't stop."

Cal jumped in, putting the sword tidily onto the heap of weapons and books and blankets and other junk under the seats. Hawk shuddered the gears, muttering to himself in exasperation. Then he said, "In the old days people knew how to travel. Horses. Fine carriages. Not these foul-stenched tin cans."

"Just because you can't afford a good one." Shadow reached out and tickled his neck. He gave a yelp; the van swerved unnervingly. Grinning, he said, "In the old days I had the best. Warhorses, chargers. Men ran out of castles to help me dismount. Squires removed my armor in sumptuous chambers, and there were women, lady, beautiful women. And feasts."

Shadow looked at Cal and rolled her eyes. He smiled back briefly, but the whole idea reminded him of Corbenic, and as the van roared up the hill the sword shifted against his foot, nudging.

Last night he had dreamed that the sword was hanging over him. He had lain there on his back in the quiet, warm room, rigid with sweat, not daring to open his eyes, and he had known, definitely, surely, with a sickening certainty, that the sword was pointing down in midair above his face, that its wickedly sharp edge was catching the glimmer from the security light on Trevor's garage, that the icy point was only just above his forehead. He had felt it descend, felt the metal touch him, pin-sharp, so that he pressed back into the pillow with a gasp and then, quickly, summoning all his courage, snapped his eyes open.

There had been nothing there.

Sick with despair, he had sat up after a while, and pulling the duvet around his shoulders, huddled in the dark. It had been at least half an hour before he'd gotten up, groped for the sword under the bed, and found it zipped safe in the canvas cover Hawk had given him. Even then he hadn't dared open the zip.

"Well, you can see why Cal doesn't want us calling for him at the house." Shadow smiled archly. "Think of the embarrassment of this thing shedding its hubcaps in such a respectable residential area. Think of what the neighbors would say!"

"Fine," Cal muttered. "Make fun."

Maybe she saw he was down, because she said gently, "I was only joking."

It was true though. He always met them at the corner. After Shadow had come to the house that first time Trevor had said, "I don't want her sort hanging round here," in a voice that Cal hated. And yet he was a bit ashamed of them himself, the van with its painted sunflowers, their terrible clothes, the mess.

Shadow was watching him in the mirror. She said, "I know

what they're like. Parents. Do what we say. Be what we want you to be." She looked away, so he saw for the first time the tiny tattooed spider that hung from the web down under her ear. "They just stifle you." She sounded surprisingly bitter. Cal nodded, wondering what she'd say if she knew he'd love to be stifled like that, to have had anyone that even cared what he did.

To his relief the van turned onto the A48. It was so noisy that talking would be a waste of time. Cal watched the winter fields. Some were plowed, others had a few sheep huddled against the cold. All the woodlands had the same stark bareness; there were no birds, except that high above Wentwood a falcon swung. He frowned, thinking of the osprey. For three weeks he'd worked at the office and washed and ironed his clothes to perfection and tried to forget about Corbenic. And despite what he'd told his mother, despite all his promises, he hadn't gone home. No money had been the first excuse, and yesterday he'd stopped her in midsentence and told her that Trevor had wanted him to work today, Saturday. It had been a lie. He just couldn't face her. He couldn't face the flat. He had only wanted to come here. He was one of the Company now, and they were teaching him. Every weekend and sometimes in the evenings Hawk practiced with him, and the moves of the sword, the dance and science of it, were coming to delight him. To his own astonishment, he loved it. He felt so much better. He was fitter;

he was sure the muscles of his arms were stronger. And he just liked being with them all.

Turning off at Catsash, the van droned painfully up the long hill. Shadow giggled. "We'd be better off pushing."

"Shut it." Hawk leaned forward, as if he urged the van on. At the top they turned left, and went through the lanes at the top of the ridge, before swinging over and down to Caerleon, where the long red curve of the Usk curled round the sprawling village. Arthur's place was just outside, down toward Llangibby. As the van pulled into the farm drive, mud from its tires spattered the lopsided gate with its chalked name. CELLI WIC FARM.

A gang of men and girls were shooting arrows at targets in the field; one of them came and opened the gate, leaning on it, and Cal saw it was the tall man, Kai.

"Well." Kai smiled his acid smile. "Our new boy. How's it going?"

"He's coming on." Hawk cursed as the engine cut out. In the sudden silence the slice and thud of the arrows, the shouts of the archers seemed unnaturally loud.

"But will he make it? There's more to being here than knowing how to swing a sword." The tall man looked at Cal narrowly. "We have to be careful."

Hawk put both brawny arms on the wheel and said quietly, "He's all right."

Kai nodded. "Let's hope so. We've had enough of traitors."

"I'll take responsibility for bringing him."

"Like last time."

Hawk started the van. "That was all a long time ago."

Kai stepped back. "As you and I both know, Hawk of May, not long enough."

The van rocked and plunged through the ruts.

"What's his problem?" Cal said irritably. "Seems like he can't stand the sight of me."

Shadow shook her head. "It's not that."

"What does he think I'm going to do?"

Concentrating on getting the van out of the mud, Hawk said grimly, "We had a lot of trouble once with someone we trusted. He almost destroyed us."

"How?" Cal asked. Shadow's kick on his ankle came just too late.

"Ask someone else." Hawk pulled up and cut the engine. He got out before Cal could say another word.

Cal looked at Shadow. "Are they really sane, these people?"

"That," she said, swinging her boots out and splashing into the mud, "I really couldn't say."

It was some sort of game, though they'd call it a reenactment. They were Arthur's Company, and they had each taken on one of the characters from the legends, and they lived it, as if they really were those people, as if they'd been alive for centuries, not in some cave asleep, but here, still living, still guarding the Island of Britain from its enemies. Sometimes he thought they really believed they were Arthur's men. Sometimes he almost believed it, too.

He spent the first hour or so that day training with Osla. Osla was built like the side of a house; he could have picked Cal up in one hand, but his gentleness was amazing. Shadow said he kept tiny canaries flying free inside his broken-down van. Osla's specialty was knife-work. He taught Cal how to defend himself, how to grab the assailant's arm, what to do against strikes. He was patient and careful.

Once, breathless, Cal leaned on the fence and said, "What about attack? When do I learn that?"

Osla didn't smile. "When I say. Arthur's men don't seek out quarrels. You have to learn about responsibility, Cal."

They were a strange bunch. Most of them seemed to live in various cottages and dilapidated barns around the farm, or in a decaying collection of vans out under the trees in the bottom field. They were always coming and going, but he'd gotten to know some of them. There was Bedwyr, a quiet man with a stutter, and a girl called Anwas, who told everyone she could fly and who spent most of her time designing bizarre machines made of plywood and feathers; there was Drwst, who had an artificial hand so strong it could straighten a bent sword; and Moren and Siawn and Caradog, all relations of Arthur's, and a poet called Taliesin and a bent ugly man called Morfran who had a brother Sandde, who they all called Angel-face because he looked like butter wouldn't melt, though he told the filthiest jokes. There was a whole clan called the Sons of Caw, about a dozen of them, all with impenetrable Glaswegian accents and looking so alike Cal could never tell which one he was talking to. There was Owein, who had a pet lion cub, and Sgilti, a whippet of a boy who could run so fast Cal told him he should train for the Olympics. Sgilti roared, and the man next to him, sharpening a pile of rusted spears, laughed with him. This was Gwrhyr, who boasted he could tell what the animals were saying, and could speak any language. If you named one he would spout a barrage of foreign-sounding words. Cal had no idea if any of it was real.

They were scruffy and dirty and they laughed a lot. But he liked them. They were like no people he'd ever met. The girls were friendly; they didn't make fun of him like the girls at home had always done. Their names were Olwen and Indeg and Esyllt, and they dressed as weirdly as Shadow, only in brighter colors. There must have been over a hundred Companions altogether, a loud, boasting, bickering tribe, who asked his name and nosed about his family and wound him up with dozens of crazy tales, how they'd once journeyed into Hell, how Gila could jump clear across Ireland in one go, how the old man Teithi had a magic knife and he could never get a handle to stay on it, and he was terrified that unless he did he'd dwindle away and die.

Kai kept them in order. Cal rarely saw him practicing any

of the arts of the Company, not jousting out in the field with Hawk, or swordplay, or archery; but his sharp sarcasms could be heard as he watched the others.

"Keep your guard up," he said to Cal, after an exhausting lesson. "Otherwise you'll get hurt. And we wouldn't want that, would we?" He was drinking what looked like wine from a glass cup, and as he turned he stepped sideways and the cup tilted. Some of the wine splashed onto Cal's white T-shirt.

"Hey!" Furious, Cal leaped back. "Be careful!"

Kai raised an eyebrow. He took out a clean silk handkerchief and tossed it over. "I'm so sorry."

Sipping, he watched Cal scrub viciously at the red stain. "It's hardly worth bothering," he said at last. "You're only making it worse."

Cal flung the handkerchief back at him. "Thanks for nothing."

As the tall man laughed and turned away, Cal sat down on the grass and dumped his sword. He was sweating and sore and angry. "Who the hell does he think he is? He did that deliberately."

"Arthur's brother." His sparring partner, a dark man called Tathal, came over, scratching his chin.

"Really?"

"Well, foster brother."

"He was in care?"

The man smiled. "Arthur was. You know, the old story."

Cal nodded wearily. "Oh, right. Sword in the stone, all that stuff. How could I forget? Don't you people ever talk about who you really are?"

Tathal ignored him. "Don't cross Kai," he said seriously. "He's our best."

"He doesn't look it. Hawk's bigger, most of the others must be stronger."

"It's not just in the body, friend. His heart is cold, and his hands. He has peculiar abilities. I mean it, Cal. He can be scary sometimes."

So can I, Cal thought wryly, watching Shadow laughing with Kai across the field, hating how tall he was, how fair, how expensive his clothes were.

He rarely saw Arthur. Later, going into the farmhouse to find something to drink, he bumped into him and Gwen coming out. He felt awkward. "Sorry. They said it would be all right . . ."

"Go anywhere you like. The house is open to everyone." Arthur's coat was worn; leather patches had been carelessly sewn over the elbows. He glanced at Cal's stained shirt; Cal went hot, but Arthur only said, "Where is that strange sword of yours, Cal?"

"Being sharpened."

"Hawk told us about the way you came by it." It was the woman, Gwen. Her hair shone in the light. "We'd like to

hear you tell that story. Have you tried to go back there, Cal?"
She was being kind, but it annoyed him. He wasn't sure they
believed any of it.

"No."

Arthur nodded, thoughtful. "It would be a good thing for
the Company to find that place. This man Bron needs help, I
think."

Cal edged past them. "Maybe . . ."

In the kitchen he drank glass after glass of water down
thirstily, while around him three men chopped and cooked
and stirred the great steamy spicy-smelling pots that held the
Company's meals. Squeezing out, he wandered into a dim,
dark-paneled room lined with books, and sank gratefully into
a chair. His legs ached and his shoulder felt as if someone had
tried to twist it off, but he felt good. For a moment he even
ignored his spoiled clothes. The Hawk had said if he worked
hard enough he might be able to fight in the Christmas event
at Caerleon, a big thing, with great crowds and a fair and a
mock medieval feast afterward for all the Company.

He was happy for at least two seconds. Then the thought
hit him hard. Christmas. He'd have to go home for Christmas.
For a moment he sat there; then he got up quickly and crossed
to the bookshelf, looking for anything that would take his
mind off her, her voice on the phone, her new hair color. *It
looks so good, Cal, I can't wait for you to see it. I've cleaned the
house, Cal, just like you like it. I can't wait to see you, Cal.*

There was a road atlas. He pulled it out and flicked the pages rapidly; then, more steadily, turned them over until he found the page with Ludlow on it. With his finger he traced the line of the railway, sitting on the arm of the chair, knees up, the book carefully balanced.

Leominster. Ludlow. Craven Arms. There was no station in between. No Corbenic. Not only that, but there was nowhere of that name all along the line, no village, no church, no hotel. He dumped the book and thought for a few seconds, then picked up the phone and dialed.

"You are through to National Rail Enquiries," a voice said brightly. "This is Alison speaking. How may I help you?"

"I want to know about trains to Corbenic."

"From?"

"Chepstow," he said at random.

There was a moment's silence, a few clicks of the keyboard. Then, "Could you spell that, please?"

He thought back to the dripping sign on the dark, lamplit platform, and said, "C-O-R-B-E-N-I-C."

"I'm sorry." She didn't sound it. "There's no station of that name listed."

"It's near Ludlow."

"I'm sorry, sir, no. Perhaps you've made a mistake?"

He nodded, then said, "Okay. Thanks."

Putting the phone down he brooded silently. Until a voice said, "That castle is not to be found in this world."

Cal jumped. Sitting in the chair opposite, his eyes bright and crazy in the sunlight, was the ragged tangle-haired man they called the Hermit.

Merlin.

·:· Twelve ·:·

The sword requires a magic spell, yet I fear you have left it behind.

Parzival

H e was eating what looked like half a cooked chicken, cracking the bones open in his hands, tearing off scraps for the dog. Cal couldn't work out why he hadn't seen him there before.

"What do you mean?" he asked after a while.

"The Grail Castle is not a place. It is a state of mind." Merlin smiled his wolfish smile. "Little apple tree."

"Have you been there?"

"I have been there."

Cal leaned forward, intent. "When?"

But a sudden distant light was in the man's eyes. "A sweet apple tree," he whispered, "growing by the river. Who eats its magical fruit now? When my reason was whole I lay at its foot. . . . I have wandered fifty years among lawless men. After wealth, after the songs of bards I have been so long in the Waste Land not even the devils can lead me astray . . ."

Cal waited. But that seemed to be all. After a few moments Merlin pulled off more of the chicken meat and chewed it calmly.

Cal tried again. "Do you know how I might find that place again?"

The Hermit looked up sharply. "Do you want to?"

Startled, Cal said, "Well . . ."

"You must wish to. With all your heart. More than life, you must wish it." Suddenly Merlin tossed the carcass to the dog and came out of the chair with a terrifying speed; he grabbed both Cal's wrists and held them tight, staring into his eyes. "And you must stop lying."

Cal tried to pull away, but the grip of the greasy hands was like iron. "I don't know . . ."

". . . what I mean? I see into you, wise fool. I see you have been hurt. All your life you have been wounded; you bleed, and you resent her for it. You will punish her for it."

"No . . ."

"You lie to them. To yourself. I know. I too have slept alone in the woods of Celyddon, and I know."

The broken nails were cutting Cal's wrists. Rigid, he said, "Let me go."

Merlin opened his hands with a strange smile. His hair was

a tangle over his eyes; the smell of him filled the room. "I see you," he whispered. "You are in a small dark cupboard, filled with rubbish. You have locked the door and you are sitting against it, all crouched up. You are not crying, but rocking back and forth. You are ten. You have a slap mark on your face. You have terrible thoughts in your heart. . . ."

Cal stood instantly. He went straight for the door and had almost reached it when Merlin said, "The way back to the Grail is long and hard. You had your chance and you didn't take it. Did you not notice, Cal, did you not see, how the Fisher King has your own face?"

Cal stopped. He put both hands out and pushed against the doorframe on each side of him, letting his breath out slowly, because it hurt him, like a sudden stitch, a stab wound. Panic crashed through him like sweat, like a chorus of voices.

When he looked up he saw Shadow. She was staring in concern. "Have you hurt yourself?"

"No," he said hoarsely.

"You look awful. Go back in and sit down."

"Not with him. He gives me the creeps."

She turned him around. There was no one else in the room.

Cal stared a moment, then crossed to the chair and looked down at it. No smell, no chicken bones. Not a dent in the cushion. "He was here."

"Who?"

"Merlin. The crazy one." He turned. "Does he live here too? Is he part of the setup?"

She sat, pulling her black hair through her fingers. "Yes. At least he has a place out in the woods; he calls it his 'moulting cage.' Hawk says it's full of feathers, and there's a pig there that he talks to. But I haven't seen him around for a while. He comes and goes. He's . . . not like the rest of us."

"Not if he can disappear into thin air he's not." But already the old, terrifying doubts were rising up in the corners of his mind, like shadows—what if he'd imagined the whole thing, talked to himself? What if these were the voices?

He turned abruptly. "Let's go outside."

They walked along the back lane of the farm, and leaned on the gate to the meadow, watching Hawk ride down and thunder lances against a swinging target that flung itself around to try and strike him on the back with its flailing ball and chain.

Cal said, "Tell me about him."

"Hawk?"

"Merlin. I don't mean the old stories—who is he? Really?"

Shadow smiled behind her cobweb. "Cal, when these people join the Company, they join it. All I know about the Hermit is that there was a battle, some terrible slaughter, and a friend of his was killed. Now don't ask me if it was a real battle or if it was some reenactment that went wrong, because it really doesn't matter in the end, whatever you might think." Ignoring his groan she went on. "He had some sort of breakdown. Went off and lived wild in the woods for years; Arthur had given up hope, but he just turned up one day and started building this den of his, this cage. He lives there most of the time, though he goes off on strange journeys."

"He talks a lot of odd stuff."

She tapped her black painted nails on the worn wood and laughed shortly. "Don't we all. But they say he's a prophet. That he knows what's to come and what's been. You have to look for the sense in what he says. Once he told me, really seriously, that the whole Company was his, not Arthur's." She turned, curious. "Did you really see him?"

"I thought I did." He caught her look and changed it to, "Yes. Of course I did. He went on about some apple tree."

Shadow laughed. "If it's not the tree, it's the pig." The dinner gong rang, whacked by one of the sweaty men from the kitchen; catching Cal's arm, Shadow pulled him toward the barn. "You'll get used to him. It's not easy, I know, being around someone like that."

As he queued for the hot soup and the greasy dollop of meat he thought bitterly that he knew far more than she did about people *like that*. He wished he could talk to her about his mother. But then he'd have to tell her she'd got it wrong, and he couldn't. He liked the idea that she thought Thérèse was his mother. But even that had its dangers. "Cal's half French," she said, at some point in a conversation he wasn't

131

listening to. He looked up, off guard, swallowing the hot soup in a painful gulp.

"Do you speak it at home?" To his horror it was Gwrhyr who asked, the one they called the Interpreter.

Cal took a hasty drink of water. "No," he said.

"Pity."

Cal grinned, embarrassed, noncommittal.

Hawk and Shadow were staying over at the farm for some sort of gathering that night. They were annoyingly secretive about it. "Don't tell me," Cal said sourly, feeling the edge of the newly sharpened sword. "The Knights of the Round Table gather to feast. I've been looking for that piece of furniture ever since I got here."

Hawk snorted. "It exists, laddie. But not like you think."

After the archery practice Shadow drove him over the hill to the Chepstow bus stop. Glancing at the clean shirt he'd borrowed she grinned. "I heard about Kai."

He scowled, silent.

"You're really anxious about keeping clean, did you know that?"

"No, I'm not."

She glanced in the mirror. "Yes you are. I saw you rearranging Hawk's books the other day. Tall ones at one end, small ones at the other. He was cursing later, trying to find something."

"I like order. Nothing wrong with that."

"Not if it doesn't get to be an obsession."

"If you knew what my house was like . . ." He'd said it before he could stop himself.

Shadow laughed. "Yes, well I've been there, remember. Talk about neat!" She grinned. "I think your father thought he'd catch something from me."

The van swung around a corner. Desperate to change the subject he said, "You're not really one of the Company yet, are you?"

"What?"

"You're like me. You're new. I can tell by the way you talk about them. And don't tell me Shadow's your real name."

She was concentrating hard on the narrow lane. Too hard. Finally she said, "No, it isn't. I was traveling on my own, out toward Gloucester, and I got into a bit of trouble. Got stranded on a road, late at night, nowhere to go. It was raining, and I was a bit scared to hitch a lift, to be honest, and I didn't know where I was going anyway. Didn't care." Her hands were tight on the wheel. He knew all the signs. "I was wet and cold and . . . well, anyway, I'd had it with everything. Then this van pulls up. With sunflowers painted on it." She grinned. "I was crazy ever to get in. I mean, total stranger. But you know Hawk."

He nodded, trying to imagine it. There was a lot she hadn't said. "So you'd left home?"

"Yes."

"They let you? Why?"

"Let's just say I couldn't get on with things at home."

She was the one sounding irritated now but he wanted to know so he waited till they stopped at the junction and said, "What sort of things?"

She glanced at him. On the wheel her hands looked oddly small, the crystals on her nails glinting. She wore frail black lace gloves with no fingers. "Look, Cal, I don't want to talk about it. Let's just say we don't all have the cozy little setup in Otter's Brook."

And then it really was hard. Not to blurt out that she'd never seen anything like Sutton Street, that he could tell from her voice that she'd been to some good school and probably had a pony and an au pair and lived in a nice little suburban place in Somerset. That she'd never had to run the house at seven years old, shopping and cleaning and holding her mother's head while she was sick and hiding the knives and hiding the bottles and all of it from the social workers and the teachers. But he kept quiet, so that when she dropped him off she said, "See you next week?"

"Sure." He opened the van door, and as he got out she said, "I wish you'd tell us what makes you so unhappy."

He stared at her in shock. "What?"

"Hawk thinks so. So does Arthur. And it's not just about Corbenic, though that has something to do with it."

He stepped back quickly. "Don't be daft! I'm fine."

For a moment she looked at him, then leaned over and

pulled the door closed. Through the open window she whispered, "Merlin was right about us both hiding." She touched the painted web on her cheek. "This isn't permanent. It can come off. But I'm not sure if yours will."

On the bus, all the way home, he brooded, obsessively picking at a tiny frayed thread on his sleeve. What was he doing with these people! Getting dirty and sweaty and learning junk about medieval warfare! He must be mad! Who did they think they were, talking about him like that, behind his back, discussing him? Hot, he looked at himself in the grimy window and swore he wouldn't go back. He'd find other friends, he thought, or do without, because they weren't anything like him. He liked things clean, and new and expensive, and he couldn't understand why he wanted to be part of their crazy setup. It wasn't him. Surely.

At the Chepstow bus station he bought some takeaway food, the cheapest he could find, as if to punish himself. While he was waiting he put the sword under one arm and stood by the window looking out into the street, ignoring the loud kids that came in, hating their tasteless clothes and filthy sneakers, hating them. Then the sword dug in his ribs, bringing him back from his annoyance.

There was a poster on the window. It was old, and people waiting had frayed its corners, and the adhesive holding it had softened so much that he could peel it off and it lay limp in his hand.

MISSING FROM HOME, it said, and there was a name, Sophie Lewis, believed to be in the South Gwent area, and an address in Bath, and a photograph of a girl in a smart school uniform smiling shyly, her light brown hair curly, her teeth in an ugly brace. For a whole minute Cal looked at it. Then he reached in his pocket and found a pencil; slowly he took it out and shaded the hair black and straight. The sodden paper tore softly; he held it together, coloring the lips a darker shade. Then, carefully, thoughtfully, he drew a cobweb over one side of her face.

"Your order, mate," the shopkeeper shouted.

Cal squeezed the paper to a tight ball and dropped it in his pocket. Some people, he thought angrily, didn't know they were born.

❖ Thirteen ❖

*Don't you think it right I should go and see my mother,
whom I left on her own in the wood called the Waste Forest?*

Conte du Graal

"Wʜᴀᴛ ɪꜱ that?" Trevor stood in front of the mirror straightening his tie.

"Opera," Cal said shortly.

Around them the music soared, deep and strange. He was getting to like it. He couldn't stop playing it.

"I know that! I mean which one?"

"*Parsifal*. It's by Wagner. German."

"Oh, the Quest for the Holy Grail. All that stuff."

Cal's pen paused over the paper. "What?"

But Trevor was absorbed in the accuracy of his tiepin. "Percival the wise fool," he said absently.

Cal sat rigid. "Who was Percival?" he whispered.

"He left his mother behind and went off to be a knight."

Trevor stepped back and studied his appearance. "Does this look straight to you?"

Cold, Cal nodded. He was doing an assignment for college, but the figures kept jumping around in his head, so he put the pen down and said, "Going out with Thérèse?"

"Business. Round Table dinner."

Cal almost snorted with laughter.

Trevor looked at him curiously. "What's got into you? And why opera? Most kids of your age are into grunge and garage and all that claptrap."

"I like the finer things," Cal said acidly.

"Like that tie."

Cal frowned. Yesterday he had had his first month's salary; he had gone into the bank and asked for the balance of his account and stared at it in delight in the porch, pushed past by irate shoppers. Then he'd deducted the rent for Trevor and it hadn't looked so great. Food for the next month. Christmas presents. And he should send something home.

But two shops down was the classy men's wear window he looked in every morning on the way to work, and he'd gone in and bought the tie. Palest gray silk. Expensive. Tasteful. Designer.

Signing the check had been a moment of real pleasure; he had taken the slim box home wrapped in tissue paper and felt buoyed up by it, happy, almost as exhilarated as when he did well in the fighting with Hawk. At last he was getting somewhere, starting to be what he wanted to be, well dressed, confident, well-off.

Thérèse had seized on the box and opened it almost as soon as he'd got into the house. For a second he had been nervous, but she had whistled and felt the silk with her carefully manicured fingers.

"Nice! Pricey?"

"A bit. But it's for work."

She had held it up to his neck. "It suits you. You always know what you want, Cal. You're like your uncle."

But he still hadn't sent any money home.

Now Trevor turned from the mirror and picked up the cream coat lying over the arm of the chair. He checked the pockets absently; watching him, Cal knew he was working out how to say something, and knew only too well what it would be. It had been coming for days.

Silver lighter, wallet, mobile phone. Trevor shrugged into the coat. Then he turned away and picked up his cashmere scarf and said it. "What are you doing about Christmas, Cal?"

At once Cal knew his mother had phoned again. He put the pen down and stared ahead. "She's rung then."

"Twice this afternoon. Look, I know how you feel." He turned, and looked away, down at the CD player. "You don't want to go back. I know, I'd feel just the same. But . . . well it's Christmas. I think you should go, just for a day or so. If you're short of the fare, I'll pay it. She's making a big effort. She's desperate to see you."

Cal was silent. A long time.

Trevor went awkwardly to the door. "Thérèse and I are going away on Christmas Eve, so you'd be stuck here on your own otherwise, and that's no fun." He turned, as if a sudden thought had struck him, and said firmly, "And I don't want those eco-warriors round here while I'm gone. That's totally, totally OUT, Cal. I have to say I wouldn't have thought they were your type."

"They're not," Cal growled. "I've finished with them."

"Good. Well ring her, will you?" Trevor opened the door and paused, fussing with his scarf. His voice was a little softer when he said, "You'll feel better when you tell her. She's your mother, after all. You owe her that much."

When he'd gone and the car had roared away the music rose from its background into a great soaring crescendo of passion.

After all, Cal thought, white with fury. After all the years of falling asleep in class because he'd been up all night waiting for her. After all the parents' evenings she hadn't gone to, the school plays she hadn't seen, all the lies, all the days she hadn't moved from the squalid sofa while the rubbish piled up around her. All the smells, the vomit, the nights under his pillow with a chair jammed against his door and next door's baby wailing and her voice, talking, answering, screaming at the nonexistent people to go away, to stop, all the arguments, the long tirades of abuse, the holidays he'd never been on, the birthdays he'd loathed, the kids in school he'd had to fight. Years of living with two people in one, never knowing who'd be there when he got home.

He hated her. For a long time he hadn't been able to think that, but he could think it now, from this distance. He hated what she'd done to his life. He wanted to love her but it was too late for that; sometime, years ago, all that had washed out of him and left a tiny hard core of bitterness and resentment and utter, cold anger. It was too late.

And Trevor couldn't talk, because he had walked out of it years ago, and never gone back.

For a long time Cal didn't move, staring ahead. Finally he looked at the phone. He ought to make the call. Tell her.

Instead he rang Sally. Her daughter answered; there was a wait, he could hear the television blaring and a baby screeching, then Sally's voice, sounding breathless. "Hi, Cal. Nice to hear from you."

"How is she, Sal?"

Sally breathed noisily. He knew she was picking her words. "Up and down, I suppose. She's on this program, and it was doing her good. Meetings. Social events, you know. I suppose . . . it's hard for her to keep it up, Cal. She's missing you, boy."

"But she's okay?" he asked desperately, wishing the answer.

"She's got you a Christmas present. Don't faint."

He closed his eyes. "That's a change," he whispered.

"And she says she's going to buy a tree."

"Oh God, don't let her."

"I'll check it, or Ryan will. We won't let her burn the place down." Then she said, "You'll be up for Christmas, Cal? She's banking on it."

And all at once he couldn't bear it anymore; his legs felt weak and his skin was cold with sweat and he said, "Yes. Of course."

He heard her silent relief. "That's great! You can come round."

He didn't want to go round. Not to talk rugby with Ryan. Not to crowd into the tiny sitting room, moving the piles of ironing. He said, "Tell her I'll ring tomorrow. Okay?"

"Is that music? God it's loud, Cal." The opera. He'd forgotten it.

"See you, Sal." The phone went down. He stared at it, face taut, hands clenched.

Then he went and flung the papers off the table, and the pens, and the file of accountancy notes, and the chessboard with its glass and silver pieces, flung them with a bitter fury all over Trevor's immaculate carpet, the chorus of singers so loud the walls seemed to shake, and he laughed, because there were no neighbors and no one to care or hear.

He threw himself down on the leather sofa. And closed his eyes.

❖ ❖ ❖

He was in a chair. A golden chair. He was sitting in the wreckage of the banqueting hall of Corbenic, and had been there forever. So long that the chair had grown roots into the ground; so long that the weeds had crept over it. As he sat there the weight of ivy was heavy on his lap, smothering his legs; its palest green tendrils had reached as high as his neck. Shuddering, appalled, he pulled it off, feeling the tear of its supple fringed growths Velcroing away from his sweater, dragging great armfuls off his chest and shoulders, and dumping them.

Then he tried to get up, and gasped in agony. Pain shot through him. It seared him, like a spear thrust. Like a heart attack. Tears blinded his eyes; he felt sick, and then the intensity of it ebbed and it was a dull, endless ache down every channel of his body, every vein. And looking down he saw that the chair had wheels.

There was a mirror. Dim, green-smeared, it showed him the room and the place where the door had been, the door the Grail had passed through, the door that didn't exist, and it showed him a man and that man was him.

Dark-haired, dark-eyed, tangled in ivy and bindweed, the ghostly white sweet-smelling flowers of it around the wheels of the chair, a man wearing his clothes, his face.

"Bron?" he whispered. And the lips of the man in the mirror whispered it too.

High in the roof, the osprey screeched. It looked down on

him with its pitiless yellow eyes, and he sat rigid, remembering the ferocity of its attack on the castle battlements.

And then Leo was there, leaning against the crumbling
doorway, arms folded.

"Now you know how it feels," he said acidly.

Cal struggled to stand. His legs had no feeling. He collapsed back in the chair, sweating, trapped in the nightmare.

"It's not me," he hissed.

"No?"

"NO!" Somewhere there was music; not the soft flutes and
harps of the Grail procession, but a wilder music, despairing,
heartbroken. It was so loud he could barely hear his own
voice as he shouted again, "NO! NO!" and then he was up
from the sofa and the opera was all around him like a crowd,
a ring of voices, the thunder of drums, the agony of violins.

In an instant he crossed the room and hit the off button.
The music stopped; then, as he turned, it burst back on,
louder, and he spun and stared at the tiny red sensor on the
CD.

"*I won't go back*," he hissed, and he turned it off again, but
it was still there; relentlessly the voices sang of their pain, of
the beauty of the Grail, its splendor, its agony, its high
enchantments, its healing.

"Stop it," he muttered, and banged the button again, then
went and tugged the plug out, smacking it against the wall.
But the music went on, it couldn't stop, it would never stop

till it reached the thundering crescendo of its chorus, and he didn't know anymore if it was real or if it was in him.

He turned and stumbled outside, slamming the door. The night was frosty. Without a coat, shivering, he ran. Out of Otter's Brook, down the dark, lamplit streets, fast, his footsteps ringing under the town arch, past the drunks on the post office steps, under the glitzy gold and red of the Christmas Santas and reindeer.

By the church he was breathless, and held on for a second to the railings. The dark bulk of the tower blotted the stars above him; gargoyles with grotesque outlines peered down. Above them a shadow flapped. Bats? The osprey?

But the music was gone. He had outrun it. Here he heard only his heart, thudding as if it would burst, and his footsteps, and as he swung into the castle car park and around the Dell he was praying, praying they'd be back, that someone would be there.

He slid and scrabbled down the mud bank.

The castle was black. But parked in front of it, with smoke coming from the jaunty tin chimney, and the sunflowers looking wan and ghostly in the starlight, was Hawk's van.

He caught his breath.

He waited a long time, getting calm, getting clean, rubbing mud from his hands, letting the sweat that soaked his back turn icy, before he walked up to the door and knocked. He was shivering, but that was the cold.

When Hawk answered he stared. "Cal. Haven't seen you for a few days."

"Been busy." He shouldered his way into the wonderfully warm interior, saw the cat on Shadow's lap, the pieces on the chessboard, the dirty dishes in the sink, the extravaganza of fabrics. The mess that he had left at home hurt his memory.

"Hi," Shadow said, surprised.

Cal turned to Hawk, urgent. "I need to train every night. I want to fight in the Christmas display. I need to, Hawk!"

Hawk folded his arms across his dirty vest. "All right. Calm down. What brought this on?"

Cal sank onto a chair and wiped the soaked hair from his forehead. "I need to be here over Christmas," he whispered.

Shadow leaned over and moved the white knight. "What he's not telling you," she said, "is that it's not that easy. You have to challenge someone first." She looked up at him then, serious behind the web of lines. "A real contest."

He shrugged, careless.

Until Hawk said, "With real weapons."

❖ Fourteen ❖

There was not a more handsome knight in all the world.

Conte du Graal

"Are you sure?" Arthur said quietly.

Cal looked down at the cracked slabs of the farmhouse floor. The kettle was boiling; Arthur waited till it switched itself off, then leaned over and poured the steamy water into all the mugs. Odd herby smells mingled.

"I'm sure," Cal said firmly.

"Is he ready?" The Company's leader looked across to Hawk, who gave a short sigh.

"Probably."

Arthur stirred his tea. "Yes or no, nephew mine."

"Yes, then. He's fast and has good control. Thinks on his feet. Parries well. Ought to build himself up more, though."

A few men laughed. Through the open window the eternal

thwock of arrows thudded into straw targets. One of the Sons of Caw drank noisily and muttered, "He could fight one of us. We wouldn't hurt him too much."

Cal frowned. He swallowed a burning mouthful of tea. Then he said, "I want to fight Kai."

No one spoke. They were all staring at him. He had a sudden frisson of terror. Then Hawk said, "No way," and Arthur, at the same time, "That won't be necessary."

"And why not?" It was Kai's voice. Even before he turned Cal knew that the fight would happen now, that he had made the challenge in front of them all and Kai could not turn it down.

The tall man had come in through the door with Shadow and Teleri and Bedwyr.

Arthur said, almost sharply, "No. He's young and foolish."

Kai laughed, a dry chuckle. "All the more reason to teach him a lesson. You heard the challenge, brother." He turned. "All of you heard it." Then he looked at Cal, came up to him, close. "Why me?" he said quietly.

Cal shrugged. He wanted to say it was because they said Kai was the best, but that wasn't the answer. And it wasn't even because he was handsome, and arrogant, or because of the Armani coat or the spoiled T-shirt. It was for a reason Cal didn't want to find. Instead he said, "Worried?" It was a mistake.

Hawk closed his eyes.

Kai's smile did not change or flicker, but for an instant there was a look to him that came and went like a cold flame.

And Arthur put the untasted tea down on the draining board and said hastily, "The challenge is given, and accepted. So be it. When do you want to begin?"

Kai turned and looked at him. "Now, brother," he said mildly.

"I didn't realize it would be today!" Cal let Hawk take his coat off him, blankly.

The big man looked grim. "God knows, Cal, what you think you're doing."

"I mean, I thought . . . a few days. A bit more practice . . ."

"Get that sweater off." Hawk turned to Shadow who came running up with the sword, hastily unzipping its case. "Gloves."

She pushed them into his hands and he shoved them onto Cal's cold fingers; long, heavy gauntlets, tied tight. "Keep your guard up," he said hurriedly. "Don't relax. He'll attack when you do. Keep a good distance; he's tall. He's fast too, so if you parry the thrust there'll be another behind it, and from an angle you won't expect. He's heavier than you, so try and use his own impetus against him. Remember . . ."

"I *can't* remember. Not all of it."

Shadow put the sword in his hands and stood back. Cal glanced, wide-eyed, at Hawk. "Where's all the protective stuff?"

Hawk shook his head, the bristle of red hair catching the low sun.

It took a second to sink in. Then Cal was appalled. "What! Nothing? That's crazy . . ." He looked down in disbelief at his neatly pressed jeans and white T-shirt. He'd be cut to pieces!

Shadow said, "You're the crazy one. Why did you have to pick Kai?"

"Because he's so bloody full of himself."

"He has every reason to be." Hawk turned him around quickly. On the far side of the muddy field Arthur's men used for jousting, an arena had been hastily cordoned off with tape. Around it the Company were gathering, running from the outbuildings.

In the middle of the space, Kai was already waiting, leaning on his sword, talking to Arthur.

Cal stumbled forward. Then he stopped dead. "What do I do? I mean, how do I win?" For a second a thought of pure terror swept over him like sweat. *Do I have to kill him?*

"You really are a fool." Hawk was stalking grimly forward. "If you stay on your feet for five minutes I'll be amazed. Get him down or disarm him. Shed blood if you must." He turned then quickly and Cal's heart sank like a stone as he caught his arm. "But listen. If it . . . if he gets ferocious, really dangerous, then throw your sword down and spread your hands wide. Back right off. Yell to Arthur that you want out."

"You mean surrender."

"That's exactly what I mean. Believe me, you'll want to."

"I can't do that . . ."

Hawk looked at him hard. Then he turned and walked on.

Cal whirled on Shadow. "I can't! I won't."

She was uneasy, fingering the blue lines of the cobweb. Finally she said quietly, "Hawk knows them better than I do. Just . . . be careful. Don't get hurt."

Fat chance, he thought, pushing past the backslapping, cheering, whistling crowd. They hustled him into the arena and closed up the line behind him and he walked out, across the muddy grass to where Arthur and Kai were waiting.

It seemed an endless walk. The wind was icy; it cut through his thin T-shirt and brought instant goose pimples prickling out on his arms, and he shivered with it, and with a sort of light-headed fear and disbelief that this was even happening. Most kids went to the pictures on Saturday afternoons, or hung around the shops. He thought of Trevor swinging a five-iron on the golf course and almost giggled, a hysterical laugh that died in his throat as Arthur said, "Are you both ready?"

He nodded. He couldn't speak. His heart was hammering and he gripped the sword tight, the corded hilt rough through the thickness of the glove.

Kai was all in black. He was smiling too, a wry, confident grin that really got Cal's back up. But then it was probably supposed to. Make him come rushing in. He wouldn't. He'd be wary.

They circled each other. The crowd yelled and whistled; a

few flakes of snow fell between them, the wind hissing over the frozen grass.

Clutching the sword, Cal watched the tall man, every nerve intent. Kai flashed out a feint attack; instantly Cal's blade went up to meet it, but there was nothing there, and he jumped back, cursing.

"Careful," Kai muttered, mocking.

Cal snapped. He knew he shouldn't but he did, dived in, struck wildly, the sword whistling through the cold air. It met a rock-hard parry; Cal pushed away but already Kai had whipped his sword around and sliced it so close to Cal's body that he had to stagger back with a gasp and yell of fear.

The crowd roared. Somewhere Shadow was shouting.

Keep his guard up. He had to! But already the sword was heavier than in practice; for a moment he knew he barely had the strength to wield it. It was growing, treacherously, in weight, and then he'd twisted and with a sudden, abrupt fury, raised it and was hacking at Kai, once, twice, thwacking into the contemptuous defense, stumbling and sweating but keeping on, forcing his opponent back, and back, the roar of the watching Company a pain in his numbed ears.

Until Kai stopped.

He chose his moment, and stopped dead, and Cal clashed into him and was held, briefly, face-to-face, sweating, gasping for breath, and he saw that Kai was still smiling, but grimly now, mirthlessly, and in that instant he knew with sickening despair that the tall man had never even been worried at all.

Then Kai shoved.

Cal stumbled back, winded, all confidence shattered.

The yells of the Company went faint: he seemed to be in a sudden realm of silence, of breathlessness and chest pain, of the harsh screeching of a bird. *The osprey.*

Panic grabbed him; he flashed a wild glance around. It was perched on the ridgepole of the farm, the great yellow beak wide, screaming at him.

Then noise surged back, roared over him, Hawk yelling, "Cal!" and Kai was on him, cutting hard, twisting, a furious energy, a devastating anger that crashed down, stroke after stroke. He parried, but his arms were numb now, each stroke weakening him, but he wouldn't give up, he wouldn't, though the mud made him slide and his breath was ragged and the gray sky was a rage of snow.

He slipped, toppled, was on his knees. Kai struck hard; the blades met with a clang that made Cal sick with the shock; it rang in his teeth and nerves. Then a blow he never even saw took his sword at a crazy angle right out of his hand and with a yell that was barely human Kai whipped his sword up high and brought it whistling down.

Cal fell. Knocked flat, he made one desperate scrabble to get up, closed his eyes, gave a gasp of terror.

And nothing happened. No crunch of metal on flesh. No agonizing blow.

Just Kai saying quietly, "I think that's enough, don't you?"

Cal opened his eyes.

Kai was leaning on his sword, grinning, not even breathless, his fair hair dark with sweat. For a moment he looked down at Cal, then held out a hand. Bewildered, Cal let himself be pulled up. Every muscle he had was aching. Blood was on his fingers.

Arthur was there, and Hawk, and he turned to them. "Is that it? It's finished?"

Arthur smiled at him. "You gave the challenge. You fought. That's all we ask."

"But . . . I lost. I didn't win." He was trembling.

Hawk groaned and threw him his sweater. "Nobody said you had to win. Nobody expected you to win."

Shivering, Cal looked at Kai, who grinned back. "It was a good fight," the tall man said. "You've got guts, though you're reckless." Then he went and picked up Cal's sword and brought it and handed it to him. "I don't know who or what you were fighting," he said, oddly quiet. "But it was more than me."

As he handed it over the sharp blade slipped in his fingers, willfully, viciously slicing his hand.

And it didn't cut him.

Before he could even think about it, Cal found himself some sort of hero. The Company swamped him with congratulations; Shadow kissed him and so did a few of the other girls, and when he had managed to struggle out of their good-natured jokes and punches he glanced up at the ridge-pole of the farm, but the osprey had gone.

"Did you see the osprey?" he asked Shadow anxiously.

She stared. "I was watching you, idiot."

"Hear it then? Screaming."

"No." Her eyes narrowed. "But that doesn't mean it wasn't there."

He scraped mud off his face with his palm, still unsteady. "You all did this deliberately. Winding me up. Making me think he was going to kill me!"

She laughed, walking backward. "You looked so scared! But you still did it."

He managed to laugh with her. Then he said, "Does this mean I get to fight at Christmas?"

"Of course." Hawk had come up; now the big man caught hold of him and marched him firmly toward the house. "You're in. On Christmas Eve you get to the Round Table at last. But I think we'd better find you a few clean clothes. You should see yourself."

Feeling the mud-plastered shirt clinging to his back, Cal grinned. Just for a moment, to his own astonishment, he didn't care.

❖ ❖ ❖

He had a shower in the farmhouse bathroom, and then Kai came in, to his surprise, and dumped a pile of clothes on a chair. "Take your pick. They'll be a bit big."

"Thanks!" Cal fingered the fine linen of one of the shirts. Then he turned quickly. "Can I ask you something?"

Kai paused, then propped himself elegantly on the side of the bath. "What?"

"The sword. It didn't cut you."

"You should keep it sharper."

"It's razor-sharp."

Kai picked up a cake of lavender soap and smelled it. "What do you expect from immortal warriors?"

"Oh, come on. You're not . . ."

"Aren't we?" The tall man smiled.

Cal scowled. "Reenactment is one thing. You lot are obsessed. Addicted. I know about people like that." He struggled angrily into a pair of trousers. "Besides, if you really were Arthur's men you'd be asleep in some cave till people needed you."

Kai flipped the soap. "Ah, the dear old cave. Trouble with that was, people always need us. They need someone to fight their nightmares for them, the dragons, the black knights. They need dreams to dream, quests to follow. Or they get trapped in the world. Like you." He stood up. "You'll have to choose a name, now. A character from the old stories." He tossed Cal the soap and went out of the door. Then he looked back in, amused. "Though Merlin says you've already got one."

Alone in the steamy room Cal stared at his own reflection in the mirror. They were all crazy, not him. He looked smart. He felt good.

He'd sort it out with his mother. New Year's—he'd go home at New Year's. He'd tell her, tonight. It would be all right.

Picking up the rest of the clothes he felt the stiffness of satin, and looked at them curiously. Doublets, medieval robes. For a moment, the glimmer of them was the glimmer and rustle of the fabrics at Corbenic. He dumped them and went out.

❖ Fifteen ❖

She has wronged me too grieviously.

Parzival

The numbers wouldn't add up. Tossing down the pen he leaned his head on his hands and yawned. He was confused and tired and bored, and to cap it all, just then Phyllis came in and said acidly, "There's a phone call for you. On your uncle's private line." It was like an accusation.

He got up wearily, and went into the other office, closing the door. He took a deep breath, picked up the receiver firmly and said, "Yes?" He still hadn't told her. He'd do it now. But it wasn't his mother.

"Is this . . . Cal?"

"That's right."

"Oh hello, Cal. I'm sorry to ring but this was the only

number I could find; I'm so glad I could get hold of you." A woman. Sounding nervous.

He sat down slowly on Trevor's chair. "Who is this?"

Some nurse. Some policewoman. But she said, "You don't know me—well, your mother may have mentioned me. My name's Rhian. I'm her case worker."

Dull relief warmed him. "Yes. She's told me about you."

"Look. I hope you don't mind me ringing. I mean, I know how it must have been for you. She's told me a few things. I know how the children . . . suffer in these cases."

"What do you want?" he said, his voice tight.

She seemed to hesitate; there was a tiny breath. "It's about Christmas."

He was chewing his nails; he made himself stop. "What?"

Then it all came out in a rush. "Cal, you will be home, won't you? I'm sure you think I'm incredibly rude for interfering like this—Annie doesn't know, of course—but it's just that she's made so much effort. She's desperate to see you. She feels . . . well she feels she's driven you away and that you can't forgive her. That you've gone like your father went."

Cal stood up, shaking with rage. "My father! What do you mean, my father!"

"Cal, I . . ."

"Who the hell are you to talk to me like this! You have no idea who I am!" His voice was raw, stammering. He didn't care.

"I'm sorry. Please . . ."

He was holding the phone so tight it hurt. "Whether or not I come home at Christmas is up to me, do you understand? *Me*. No one else! No bloody social worker!"

"It's for your mother, Cal. That's the only reason I'm asking you. I know I've upset you. I'm sorry. It was clumsy. All I want to know is that you're coming. I really think that if you don't come she'll relapse."

That sweet, sincere tone. He'd heard it so often it turned him sick.

"That'll be my fault, will it!"

"Of course not. It's just . . ."

"Well you needn't bother worrying. I'm coming home on Christmas Eve. Now get off my bloody back!" He crashed the phone down hard. For a moment he stood there breathing deep. Behind him the door creaked. Phyllis had made sure she had heard every word.

He swung around, grabbed his coat, and slammed out of the office.

Chepstow was cold, frosty. It was four days to Christmas and the schools had broken up; kids were in the shops, and outside Boots a tiny merry-go-round purred round and round, empty except for one little boy sitting on his mother's lap and laughing. All the windows were lit with fairy lights and tinselly decorations that reflected hundreds of tiny colored glimmers into Cal's eyes. Hot with rage he walked through them all, then found himself staring in at Oxfam's old clothes, clutching his arms tight around his body, his mind saying, "Money. I'll send money," over and over.

Slowly, he made himself cool down. Getting worked up didn't help. He had to control it. His training with Hawk had helped him see that.

There was another of the MISSING posters on the Oxfam window. He reached out for it but it was inside, so he touched only glass.

Sophie Lewis. It was her. He should warn her about them. How could she hate what he had always wanted? How could a big house and private school and skiing holidays be hell? *What did she know about hell?*

When he got home he was surprised to hear Thérèse humming in the kitchen. The immaculate living room was rich with the smells of cooking; Cal knew Trevor would be annoyed about that.

He had meant to march straight upstairs and put the opera on, to slam his door and lie buried in the music of the Grail but Thérèse put her head out and said, "Coffee?"

Cal sank onto the cream sofa. "Thanks." But if she mentioned Christmas, he thought . . .

She brought it out on a tray, with two delicate cups and some almond biscuits. It smelled as he thought France must smell. One day, when he'd made his money . . .

Thérèse poured from the cafetière and added a splash of hot milk. She sat back and curled her feet up luxuriously. Perhaps she saw he was upset; she sipped the coffee and was quiet for a while, and then said, "Trevor phoned. His client was late. We're dining in tonight. For a change."

He nodded, scratching absently at a tiny mark in the blond wood.

"Join us, Cal. We've barely eaten with you since you came."

He smiled, wan. "I thought I'd go to Hawk's."

"Your New Age friends?"

He nodded.

"You like them?"

"Yes," he said simply.

She smiled. "I did too. That girl, I liked her." She leaned over. "Don't take any notice of what Trevor says, Cal. Friends are important."

He rubbed the warm cup between his hands. "Are you going to marry him?" he asked quietly.

Thérèse didn't seem surprised. Her dark, curly hair had come loose and a trail of it curled on the fluffy sweater she wore. After a moment she said, "Trevor is . . . different from me. I love him, he's a dear. But . . ."

"He's too tidy."

It was a joke, but she didn't laugh. Instead she said sadly, "He doesn't want children."

Cal was silent. No, he thought. Not Trevor. Not a crying

baby, not all the mess, the sickness, the toys, the greasy finger-marks on the furniture. Not all the upheaval in this perfect life he'd made for himself.

"But you do?"

She smiled. "I do, Cal. And I want a warm, messy kitchen and flowers and a grubby dog and dirty wellingtons and a real log fire."

He nodded, and drank the coffee. She said, "You're like him."

"No, I'm not."

"Yes, you are, chéri. But don't be too like him, Cal. Some-thing died in him, long ago. Don't let it die in you too."

Embarrassed, he put the cup down and took one of the biscuits. To change the subject, abruptly he said, "She's run away from home, did you know? Shadow. There are posters round the town. She should be in Bath doing A levels."

"No!" Thérèse sat up. "But that's terrible. Her parents must be frantic! You must tell her to go home, Cal. After all, it's Christmas, no? How could she do that to them?"

It stung him. He put the biscuit down, untouched.

Trevor's key rattled suddenly in the lock.

"Don't tell him," he whispered urgently. "About Shadow."

She nodded, reluctant. "Promise me you'll talk to her."

"I will," he muttered.

But it was only after they'd seen the overcooked, crusty ruin of the pizza and Hawk had groaned and threatened the microwave with a battle-axe that he knew he would do it.

Hawk got up, his bristly head brushing the van roof. "That's it. Chips. Fish. For three?"

Cal nodded and thought with a sigh of Thérèse's French cuisine. It reminded him. But when Hawk had gone, Shadow said, "Will your parents mind?"

"Mind what?"

"You being with the Company. It'll be at night, Christmas Eve, late. At Caerleon."

"I'm not a kid," he said crossly. Then, "Will you be there?"

"Of course." She tied her slick hair back in a sliver of dark lace. "I get to join up too."

"Girls? At the Round Table?"

She grinned, smug. "Maybe they've changed with the times." As she turned, her long skirt brushed the table and toppled it; knives and forks slid off, a scatter of pens, a whole pack of cards. Cal bent instantly, but her black, gloved fingers caught his arm. "Leave them."

"But . . ." He stared. "Why?"

"Because I say." She sat opposite, watching him. "I just want you to leave them there. If it doesn't bother you."

"No." He sat back, his feet among the cards. "Of course it doesn't."

But it did. The cat jumped up on his lap; he pushed it down and said, "Shadow . . ."

"Just leave the stuff on the floor, Cal." She leaned

forward. "It's just untidy. It's not hurting."

It hurt him. He couldn't breathe; he knew she was trying him, that it was some sort of test and he couldn't stand it so he said, "There are posters about you. All over the town."

"Posters?" Her look was suddenly alert, her skin white under the cobweb.

"Missing from home. Sophie Lewis."

"Oh, God!" she said, jumping up. "Will Hawk see them?"

"There was one in the chippie. But I took it." He held out the crumpled ball; it had dried hard and broke as she pulled it open. She read it, then flung the scraps in the tiny stove, turning on him in rage. "Why didn't you tell me!"

"I'm telling you now. Doesn't Hawk know?"

"Of course not!" She was standing now, restless in the cramped space. "I mean, he doesn't know they're looking for me. He thinks it's okay."

Cal nodded. Carefully he said, "Maybe . . . you should phone. Just tell them you're well."

"I've done that. My mother just goes on. I can't stand it."

He looked down.

"You wouldn't understand!" she burst out. "Sure, I had everything I wanted. Good home, school, clothes. But I hated it, Cal, because no one gave a damn about me. The real me, not what they wanted me to be. A family, that's what I was searching for. And I found one. Hawk—he's great, but my parents would detest him. I mean, come on, no money, no old school tie, nothing. Just some pathetic person who lives in the past!"

He wanted to interrupt, to say something but she swept on, grabbing a handful of the tablecloth and twisting it in her fingers. "They just want me to do it all their way. Go to university. Get a high-powered job. Become a barrister or a stockbroker. There's this boy, Marcus, he's cracked about me. His father plays golf with mine. He's all right but I know what they're thinking. His father's money, their company. Get married. Have kids. I wanted to break out, smash out, right out of that life. The stink of their money."

"What's wrong with money?" he said, sullen.

"Plenty. These people, Hawk, Arthur, they don't care about money. It's like a new world for me." She looked down at him. "Listen. Don't tell Hawk. Or any of them. They'd never let me join them, they'd just send me home. No one knows but you. And Merlin, though I certainly never told him."

"It's not fair on Hawk."

She shrugged, stubborn. "That's my business."

"And look, Shadow, it's not fair on your parents." Suddenly it mattered to him that she went, that one of them went back, and he couldn't, he couldn't, so it had to be her. "Think what sort of a Christmas they're going to have!" He stood up, and to her shock she saw his eyes were wet. "Think of them alone in that house, and how they'll be thinking of you, only about you! How can you do that to them! How she'll be crying, all by herself. Drinking. Thinking you hate her. Knowing you hate her."

"I don't hate them!"

"They won't know that!"

He caught her wrist; amazed, she shook him off. "Get lost, Cal! Get off my back! This is my problem! It's got nothing to do with you!"

For a second he stared at her as if there was something huge he had to say, something so massive it would destroy him to speak it. Then he had turned and gone, brushing past Hawk so that a packet of chips fell on the frozen soil.

"Hey!" Hawk yelled. "What's the rush?"

Cal glanced back at Shadow's stricken face. "I'll see you on Christmas Eve," he whispered.

On the twenty-third he packed.

When his mother rang he said bleakly, "I'll be home tomorrow. The train gets in about six."

"Oh God, Cal, it'll be so good to see you."

Her voice was husky; he had to loosen his grip on the phone, and say, "I haven't been away that long."

"It seems like forever!"

He knew she had been drinking. Years of interpreting her mood, the nuances of her voice, told him that. Not much, but enough.

"Mam," he said quietly, "are the voices still gone?"

She was silent. Then her whisper came, secret and confiding. "Last night, I heard them. At first I thought it was him and her next door, arguing, but it wasn't. It was a lot of people, Cal, like a great crowd, somewhere far off, laughing and talking, and a clatter like plates and dishes. A banquet. And music, faint, like harps. And you were there, Cal."

"Me?"

"I heard you. As if you were close to me. '*I didn't see a thing,*' you were saying, loud, like you do when you're getting all het up."

He stared across the room at the mirror, at himself. "You can't have," he whispered.

But her mood had changed; she was scared now. "I haven't heard them for so long. When they'd gone, I got up and went in all the rooms, and sat on your bed—it's so tidy, Cal, spotless, just like you keep it—and I listened. All night I listened. But they didn't come back. Will they come back, Cal? Like they used to do?"

"I don't know," he said desperately. Then, "No. Not if you remember to take your pills. You are taking them, aren't you?"

"The dustbin worries me." Her voice was thin now, full of dread. "It keeps overflowing. I can't remember when they come for it."

"Thursdays." He was sweating; he said, "Ask Sally. She knows. Look, I've got to go now. I'll see you tomorrow. Tell this woman Rhian about the voices. Ring her now. Don't forget. And Mam . . ."

"You are coming? If you don't . . ."

"I've SAID! I've said I'll come." He calmed his voice, with an effort. "Okay?"

"Okay," she whispered.

"Mam . . ."

"What, sweetheart?"

Don't drink anything. Stay out of the pub. Walk the long way round, away from the off-license. Stop blackmailing me. Stop ruining my life.

But all he said was, "I'll see you tomorrow."

"I love you, Cal," she whispered.

He put the phone down and sat with his head in his hands. He sat there for an hour, then went up to his bedroom and closed the door and pulled the duvet off the bed and wrapped it around himself, huddled against the radiator, trying to get warm, to let the darkness cover him, to make the whole sickening mess go away.

He had to go. He had to go. But if he did he had to tell Hawk he wouldn't be at Caerleon, and he wanted so much to be with them, all of them, in the cheerful, messy farmhouse. All his life all he had ever wanted was to be normal, have a family, real friends.

Through the night in the silent house his thoughts tormented him, trapped in the endless agony of his selfishness, of his dread. He must have slept, because at some point the whole mess liquefied, became a whirlpool sweeping him down, into the golden hollow of a great cup, and he was scrambling hopelessly to climb out, but the sides were slippery and sheer and he fell back with a splash.

And there were all sorts of things with him in the red flood; Shadow was there with her face paint washed off, and Hawk, clinging to the wreckage of his shield, and Phyllis, swimming firmly with strong strokes.

"Little apple tree!" A voice hissed above him, and he looked up and saw Merlin. The madman was balanced, feet wide, on the lip of the cup; now he squatted and held out a long, shining lance and said, "Catch hold, knight. For the quest begins here. Here the marvels begin; here begin the terrors!"

With a great effort Cal flung his arm up and grabbed the lance, but his clutching fingers slid on it, and he saw that it was bleeding, great drops of blood, and it was the blood that filled the cup, the blood that was drowning him.

He let go, and fell, down and down, and the darkness came up around him, and it was sleep.

"Have a good time." Cal leaned into the car.

"Thanks," Thérèse said happily. "And give your mother my love."

Trevor was fishing in his pocket. He brought out a small package. "This is for her," he said. "Tell her . . . tell her Happy Christmas from me."

Cal took it silently. Behind him the station announcements echoed. He turned. "I'd better go."

For a second all he wanted to do was get back in the car. Thérèse put her hand on his arm. "It will be all right," she said quietly. "As soon as you get there you will enjoy it. And it's only for a few days. Think what it means to her, Cal."

He nodded.

As the car turned in the forecourt and drove away he waved, seeing Thérèse's hand waving back until they turned the corner and were gone. Then he picked up his bag and went into the station.

He got into the queue for the tickets but when he was two from the front he turned abruptly and went on to the station and sat on a bench, cold to his bones.

The station clock said nine twenty. At ten twenty he was still there. Trains came in and went out. Announcements echoed, reverberating lists of names and places he'd never been. People got on and off, kissed good-bye, bought newspapers, ran. Ordinary people. People going home for Christmas.

He was frozen; he couldn't move. He watched them without curiosity, as if all feeling had drained out of him. As if he was invisible among them.

When the third train for Newport had left, the platform was empty. He stood up, numb with exhaustion.

Then he went home. To Otter's Brook.

❖ Sixteen ❖

She greeted Arthur and all his household save Peredur.
And to Peredur she spoke wrathful, ugly words.

Peredur

He slept all day.

At six o'clock, bleary and rigidly careful, he dressed in crisp
clean jeans, a pale shirt, a warm pullover, his dark jacket. He
ate some cold meat and pickles that were in the fridge,
washed up, tidied every object in every room, hoovered,
rearranged Trevor's Christmas cards in fanatical order of
height and left a note for him on the dustless windowsill.

Hawk and Shadow were meeting him at seven. But first,
he had to make that call. It took him five minutes to summon
the strength to pick up the phone. Then, cold with fear, he
grabbed it and rang his mother. "I can't get there," he said
quickly, hurriedly. As if saying it fast would help, would make
it easier for her. "The trains were all running late, and I got as

172

far as Newport, but then the next two were canceled. Christmas, I suppose. Too many people."

She was silent.

He said, "Are you okay?"

"Yes." It was very small, barely there.

"I'll come after Christmas. I promise I will." As he said it he believed it, and his heart went light and happy. Why not? He'd be part of the Company, it would be done, and he could go. Just for a few days. "And I'll stay till New Year. You can show me all the things you've done. We can go out for a meal . . . it'll be great."

Another silence. Then she said, "All right, Cal."

It wasn't enough. He needed more. He needed anything, even screaming. He was suddenly, breathlessly terrified. "Will you go to Sally's? They'd love to have you for Christmas dinner. Or Rhian?"

"Rhian's got her family," she said. Her voice was distant, as if the line was failing. "I'll be fine, Cal."

"I'll ring you. First thing. Wish you Happy Christmas. I've got a present to give you from Trevor too."

There was a small breath and a crackle. Did she believe him? What was she thinking?

"I love you, Cal." She whispered it like she always did. Then she put the phone down.

He sat there, cold and still, hearing the purr at the other end, listening to it for long moments, before he put the receiver on his lap and rubbed his face with his hands, hard, up into his wet hair. He hated himself. For a terrible instant he thought the guilt would be too much for him, too heavy. And then he told himself it would be all right. Just a day. One day.

He went for a drink of water, downed it in one go, came back and pressed the button and redialed.

"Chepstow Police," a man said.

Cal swallowed. "The girl on the posters," he said quickly, in a clipped, hard voice. "Sophie Lewis, the one that's missing. She's living in a van parked up most nights in the Dell, by the castle. Tonight she'll be at the pageant, at Caerleon. She's dyed her hair black, and there's a tattoo on her face."

"Can I have your name . . . ?" The voice was quick but he cut it off, and on a sudden impulse of disgust flung the phone away from him onto the sofa so it bounced and the receiver fell off.

He walked rapidly to the door. But before he'd got three steps he had to come back and tidy the place up.

The night was frosty; all the stars brilliant.

In Caerleon strings of lightbulbs swung over the dark streets; as the van rattled past the museum and down the lane onto the barracks field, Cal saw that all the vans of the Company were parked there, and as Shadow opened the door and jumped out the smell of woodsmoke and trampled grass made Hawk grin.

"Give us a hand," he said, dragging out swords and hel-mets and shields. Shadow ran around to help him, laughing.

Her laugh made Cal feel sick at what he'd done. But it was for the best. One day she'd thank him.

He found his own sword, and took it out of the case. It shone in the blue light.

The event for the public was fun, but short. Bonfires burned on the field; among them in the cold wind the Company staged a mock tournament and then a melee, with everyone fighting with swords and axes, pretending to be cut down, the audience clapping and drinking and balancing hot sausages and burgers.

Lying curled on the grass, breathless, Cal grinned to him-self. For a second he forgot the whole world with the pleasure of being here, being part of something, the easy jokes, the friendly banter.

Until Kai came around and kicked his leg and said, "Get up, hero. It's all over."

He struggled up, and found he was cold. And sore. And muddy. At least he was wearing a costume, a grubby chain mail. As he thought it, he saw the crowd was thinning, the people traipsing to their cars, going home to warm Christmas Eves in decorated houses, the children put to bed early, too excited to sleep. In churches there would be singing, and masses, and small models of the crib. Tomorrow the whole Company would attend. Arthur insisted on it.

It was the children he envied. Brushing himself down,

gathering up the sword, he let himself think of his own past Christmases, saw himself small in bed, hoping each year things would be different, things would be like the families in books, on TV advertisements, that there would be presents and a good, hot dinner and that the house would be magically warm and comfortable and that his mother would be a different person. It made him sick now, and angry.

"It does not do," Merlin said next to him, "to be too sorry for oneself."

Cal turned, sword in hand.

"Stop creeping up on me! Where the hell did you come from?"

The Hermit's patchwork coat was thick with mud. He reached out and touched the sword, deliberately stroking its sharp edge, his hand thin and filthy, with bitten nails. Cal jerked away. "Be careful!" Behind him, the dog whimpered.

"I brought you to the Company," Merlin whispered. "The dark knights that once attacked you were conjured by me."

"Conjured?"

"Spirits at my command. I guide the Company; I move its fortunes as I moved the great stones once." He nodded, then put his lean hand on Cal's shoulder. "Look for me when things are darkest. You and I, knight, will journey together. We will sleep alone in the woods of Celyddon, shield on shoulders, sword on thigh. When all but shame deserts you, look for me."

Cal stared at him, sick, shaking. But the man was already walking away, and Cal saw how he turned and yelled in fury at the dog, and how it followed, patient, unmoved.

It was late now; nearly midnight. In the ruins of the Roman amphitheater, all around the high green banks, the Company waited, as if they had gathered from all over Britain for this night, this moment. As he walked with Shadow onto the dim, flame-lit circle of trodden arena, Cal picked out faces he knew: Hawk, Kai, Gwrhyr, Owein, and others that were strange to him, men and women of all ages and sizes, dressed in bizarre mixtures of clothes, half-glimpsed, beyond the ring of crackling, shockingly scarlet flames that flattened and leaped and roared in the wind.

Before him, seated on a simple bench, Arthur waited, though instead of his usual tweed he wore armor now, a strange, semi-Roman breastplate, dinted and battered from old blows, and a white cloak that seemed ghostly under the eerie light, because the moon had risen, a thin crescent over Wentwood, and it glimmered on the cold edge of the sword.

Arthur stood, and said quietly, "Welcome to the Round Table, Cal."

Cal shook his head. "I thought . . ."

"Yes. Well, no piece of furniture would be big enough." Arthur turned to Shadow. "And you. Are you ready to join us?"

"Yes." Her voice was low; Cal saw her hands were clasped

tight together, black fingers with small silver rings over the gloves, and a faint silver thread embroidered there. She glanced quickly at him; the cobweb a dark mask over one eye.

If he was lying, he thought, if he was betraying them, then so was she.

Arthur raised his voice. "Friends! Does the Company of the Island of the Mighty accept these two among us?"

There was a murmur of consent, and a yell from Hawk that made Shadow giggle.

Arthur held out his hands for the sword; Cal laid it across his palms. "Now, both of you, put your hands on it."

Shadow's fingers lay on the blade; Cal put his fingers beside hers, feeling ridiculous and grave and afraid all at once.

"You must swear loyalty to me," Arthur said. "But first tell me that you have no dishonor in your hearts."

That shook Cal. His fingers went icy on the pale steel. And how could Shadow say, "None," like she did, so calm, so quiet?

Arthur looked at him. For an instant Cal thought of his mother, sitting on the sofa in the cold house. Of the new Christmas tree. It would be lopsided. She'd never have been able to make a good job of it on her own.

"None," he whispered.

The flames crackled and spat. The wind roared.

Arthur said, "Then take your sword, Cal." He stepped back, leaving them both holding it between them, heavy, wickedly sharp, gleaming.

And it snapped. With a crack that rang in the broken walls and tunnels and hollows of the amphitheater, the sword broke itself in two, vindictively, spitefully, and Cal staggered with the sudden shock of it, Shadow's stifled scream, the words that hissed out of the dark. "*It will serve you as you have served me.*"

For a moment of terror he knew these were the voices; then he turned, and saw her standing there, the girl who had carried the Grail. She was wearing the same long dress, her hair braided up, but her face had changed; it was old now, so ugly, wrinkled, and heavily lidded that he would hardly have known her.

Horrified, he staggered back; Arthur caught his arm and said, "Who are you?"

The old woman's smile was sour. "Hear me, King." She turned, raising her voice. "Hear me, you, Arthur's men."

Kai was shouting orders; Hawk leaped down into the arena.

"Don't listen," Cal hissed desperately. "I don't know her."

Her finger stabbed at him. "Here is one who has betrayed you! Here is one who saw the holy things, and could not ask about them, not what the cup contains or who drinks from it! Who didn't care why the lance bleeds! Here is one who denied they ever existed!" She turned around and glared at him, and to his terror her face flickered in the flame light, young and old, ugly and beautiful, as if the red glimmer of the light and the wind redefined it, and he knew it, and then

179

it was strange, it changed as his mother changed, minute by minute.

Arthur made a swift downward jab with his hand; the men running toward him slowed, wary. "We know about this. But the boy is young; he . . ."

"You do not know the reason for his failure." She was speaking to Cal now. "He cannot make a new life on the ruins of the old. There is a thing he has left undone. Unsaid. A weight on his soul. A woman he has abandoned. Until he goes to her and heals himself he will never find the Grail. And the Waste Land will remain waste, and the Fisher King will suffer his endless pain." She spat at him; he jumped back. "He is a fool," she hissed. "He has failed."

The wind roared; a police siren echoed far off in the village. From the church, suddenly, joyously, the bells began to ring, a clashing, jangling frostiness of sound. It was midnight. It was Christmas.

"Who does she mean? Who is this?" Arthur was asking.

Cal swallowed. It was impossible to say the words but in sheer despair he said them. "My mother," he whispered.

Shadow said, "Thérèse?"

He turned to her. "Not Thérèse." The siren was loud now, the car racing up to the amphitheater, stopping with a squeal of brakes.

"I'm sorry," he whispered, to her, to all of them.

"What?" Wary, Shadow glanced around, backed off. "Have

you told the police about me? *What have you done, Cal?*"

The woman was going, turning and walking into the dark, and in her hands he saw she held a shape of darkness, veiled and hidden. From the entrance tunnel voices rang, angry, until Arthur roared, "Let them through!" his breath smoking in the frosty air.

Two figures. Running. A man and a woman.

"Don't blame me," Cal said miserably, clutching the sword. "I thought it was for the best. I did it for you. I'm sorry, Shadow."

"You stupid, *stupid* fool!" she hissed.

The bells stopped instantly. And suddenly in the terrible silence, across the frosty field he saw that the man was Trevor, and the woman, breathless, one high-heeled shoe slipping off, was Thérèse.

Trevor grabbed him. "Cal! Thank God!"

"What? What is it?" He was icy with fear. Shivering, sweating with fear.

Trevor glanced at Arthur, then back. His face was aged and stricken in the red flames. "It's your mother."

"What!" In agony Cal flung the broken sword down. "What? For God's sake tell me! *Tell me!*"

But it was Thérèse who came up and put her arms around him. It was Thérèse who told him that his mother was dead.

✳ Stone ✳

✳ Seventeen ✳

For when thou didst set out against her will,
pain leapt up in her . . .

Peredur

He edged the dusty net curtain aside and watched the
street. Kids were in a gang on the corner, arguing. They
climbed and perched on the old settee that was rotting there,
absorbed totally in whatever the fight was about. One of
them lit a cigarette, throwing the match down the drain. It
amazed him that people could go on, as if nothing had happened. As if she was still alive.

The first night, with Trevor hushing the neighbors away
into the back room, he had sat here and stared at the six
o'clock news, waiting for the item to come up: woman,
found dead in Bangor, the pills, the bottles of spirits. It
hadn't. It wasn't important. It probably happened somewhere
every day.

Now the taxi was turning the corner. It came up past the kids and crawled, looking for the number.

Cal glanced around, suddenly panicky. The room was quite empty, all the flat was. It looked stark and tiny and grubby; he could hardly believe all his life had been spent between these walls. He had a feeling he should be sentimental now, go around saying good-bye to places, like the room where . . . her room. But he couldn't. He hated the place more than ever. He would never have to see it again.

Quickly, he picked up the rucksack and went outside, closing the front door with a clap, sending a few more flakes of its blistered paint scattering.

Sally must have been looking out; she was waiting by the taxi, and to Cal's embarrassment she put her arms around him and squashed him to her. She was big, and smelled of soap.

"Bye, Sal," he muttered.

Her eyes were red. "Look after yourself, boy. Give us a ring now and then, we'd be glad to hear from you, Cal. Don't forget all about us."

"No," he said dully. He didn't know what he meant by it. She was looking at him as if he was small and lost and he was and he couldn't let her know, so he straightened up and got in the taxi and said, "The station," as coldly as he could.

"Right, mate." The taxi jerked and reversed and pulled away. Sally waved. He made himself wave back.

But once around the corner he sank into the seat,

exhausted, as if some tacky elastic cord had snapped, and he was free. He couldn't feel anything. He was numb.

There had been the funeral, in the big, cold church she had only gone to when she had nowhere else to go, and the cold rain in the cemetery, and all the neighbors looking at him. If it hadn't been for Thérèse he'd never have gone through with it. They were all sorry, they said, but he knew what they thought. They blamed him. Going off, leaving her. They looked at his new work suit and the gray silk tie and they despised him. They were right to.

"Don't blame yourself," Thérèse had said. She meant well.

The inquest had been worse. Rhian had given evidence, a pretty woman with brown hair, flustered; she had come up to Cal after and said, "I'm so sorry," and he'd thought that she didn't know, did she, that no one knew except Trevor and Thérèse that he had killed her. That his staying away had killed her.

There had been doctors, and Sally and then Trevor, and the verdict had been left open, not even suicide, because she was so absentminded, Sally had said, and she might not have known she was taking too many. And she'd been drinking.

"Unfortunate," the coroner had said. "An unfortunate and tragic event, and our sympathies to the family, especially her son."

"Three pounds, mate," the taxi driver said again, patiently.

Cal paid, got out, went into the station, sat and waited

without thinking, staring at the advertisements on the wall, reading them over and over and not seeing them.

After Thérèse had left he and Trevor had cleared the flat. There had been the lopsided Christmas decorations to take down, and the tree, but Trevor had done that, because Cal had had to go out, away from it. She had tried. It was the trying that hurt him most.

Most of the furniture was cheap and worthless. Trevor had put an apron on and worked all day, grimly, barely speaking, phoning charity shops and dealers, getting everything sold: her clothes, the cups and saucers, the junk in the cupboards. His distaste had been silent and bitter. Cal had burned with shame at the mess.

"Take anything you want, mind," Trevor had kept saying, and Cal had fingered old schoolbooks and smelled her cardigans, but there was nothing here he wanted.

Except, at the back of her bedside drawer, there was a picture he had drawn when he was about five, for Mother's Day. The straggling writing was huge, copied from someone else at school, probably. *Have a Happy Day Mummy.* He had never called her that. Almost, he had cried then. A hot lump had come in his throat and his eyes had gone sore, but Trevor had called from downstairs, and he had rubbed his face and swallowed the lump and pushed the card into his rucksack. It hurt him. Like a wound. He didn't know why he was keeping it.

The train came in and he got on it, and all morning he watched the woods and mountains and the tiny newborn sheep in the frosty fields, and the great expanses of sea at Rhyl and Colwyn Bay. People sat by him and came and went; he had a newspaper but he couldn't read it, and finally at Crewe he got out and found himself sitting on the red metal seat on the platform reading the destinations board stupidly, as if he had been traveling forever and had never even started out.

She had killed herself. Sometimes he was sure of that, despite what the coroner had said; he imagined the scene in every detail, the Christmas tree, the bottles on the table. The pills. Her hands, taking one after another, deliberately, shakily. Her hands holding the cup. Sipping. And then, straight afterward, he wasn't sure; it could have been an accident, she was drunk, she could easily have forgotten she'd already taken them. It was a nightmare seesaw of thoughts that he couldn't get off.

Trevor had gone back to work two days ago, and Cal had had to stay in Bangor till everything was sold and the landlord had had the keys. Now there was nothing to go back for.

As the train rattled down through Cheshire and into the hills of Shropshire he knew that he was free, but the release of that was tiny against the terrible, cold stab of blame. It was his fault. And her fault. She had spoiled everything forever. He would never be free of her now; the blame and the shame of it would ruin his life, as she'd ruined it when she was alive, as she'd always ruined everything. It was too hard to think of; he hated himself. He got up and grabbed his rucksack and shouldered past the drinks trolley ferociously, down the carriage to the door and he had hold of the door and was pulling it and pulling it, just to get some air, to get away from the thoughts, to get out.

"Son." A hand on his arm. "Son. Take it easy. The door's locked." The guard. Two women behind him, looking scared and concerned. A whole carriage of horrified faces.

Cal took his hands off the door and stepped back. He was shaking, his back wet with sweat.

The guard said, "It's okay." He had hold of Cal; Cal went weak at the knees.

The guard flipped down the overflow seat and turned quickly. "Get him some tea," he said.

The train rattled over points, swung through a long curve. Trees flashed past the windows.

Cal couldn't speak. He was shaking too much, and the guard crouched down in front of him and said, "Drink this, son. You look done in." It was a white plastic cup, and when he sipped from it the hot tea hit him like a blow, and his ears seemed to pop, so he heard the words from the women behind, the words *shock* and *suicide*.

"Better?"

He said, "I wasn't . . . I forgot we were moving." It sounded crazy.

189

The guard said, "Whatever you say, son. How far are you going? Is anyone meeting you?"

"Corbenic," he said. Then, confused, "Chepstow."

The guard nodded. Suddenly Cal was alarmed. Would he radio ahead, would Trevor hear about this? With a terrible effort he stood up and said normally, "I'm sorry. I really thought the train had stopped. Half asleep, I suppose." He tried to smile. Maybe it looked all right because the guard got up too, his knees creaking.

"It's two hours to Newport. You change there. Maybe you should have some more sleep."

When they'd left him alone, and the two women had gone back to their seats, Cal sat by the window and stared out at his own reflection over the flashing fields.

The cup. He looked down at it, an empty plastic cup, and would have crushed it in his hand, only that it would make loud cracking noises and people would look at him again. If he had opened that door and fallen out . . .

He closed his eyes. He had to be careful. Follow the rules. Not panic. But the rules were shattered and useless and he knew that his shirt was dirty and his trousers scruffy and he hadn't even thought about anything like that for days.

The cup. That's what he would do; he would find the cup. That shining Grail, that feeling it had given him. He had failed her, but he wouldn't fail at this. And for a moment he almost thought that if he could find the Grail it would bring her back somehow, it might help, might cure the hurt, not just for Bron but for him. There was nothing to go back to Chepstow for; Shadow would have been found by now, she'd despise him, and the Company . . . he had lied to them. He hated his job; only now could he see clearly that it wasn't for him, that he only endured it for the money. Why had he ever thought he could do that for the rest of his life?

The guard was passing. "Okay now?" Keeping an eye, Cal thought.

"Fine. What's the next station?"

"Ludlow. Ten minutes."

It was here. Somewhere. Out there in that green wasteland of woods and rivers and hidden valleys, of castles and factories and hills. Corbenic was out there, and he would find it. It would be his quest. And Ludlow would be as good a place as anywhere to start.

He made no move till the train hissed in and stopped; then when the doors had whished open he grabbed his rucksack and stepped out. Cold air enveloped him.

"Hey!" At the front end of the train the guard was waving. "Son! Not your stop!"

Cal ignored him. He waved, turned, and walked up the steps quickly, over the little bridge, down the other side. There was a street leading past a big new supermarket; he went down it, and into the town. Shops. Old black-and-white inns. A few market stalls.

He went into a café and bought a coffee, and asked the girl who brought it if she knew a place nearby called Corbenic.

"No, sorry." She looked at him shyly. "But you could try the library. They've got maps."

He nodded, stirring the sugar in.

It was not on any map. After a good hour of searching he sat with both hands on the wooden desk, feeling lost and worn out. There was no such place as Corbenic. Or as Merlin had said, it wasn't to be found on the map.

He picked the rucksack up and wandered outside, and found it was dark. The shops had closed, and a faint icy rain was falling, spotting the pavements, soaking his hair quickly. He walked on. He was in a strange town, alone, at twilight, with no idea where he was going or what he was doing, but he wouldn't give up. Because this was the quest; this was where it began. The descent, the marvels, the terrors. His penance.

He found a hotel on the main street; there was a phone box in the lobby and he rang Otter's Brook and Trevor answered.

"Hi," Cal said quietly.

"Where are you?"

"Still in Bangor." *Still lying.* "Look, I've got a few friends to see, and then . . . well, I thought I'd take a bit of a break, if you don't mind."

He could feel Trevor's sigh. "Well, I suppose a few days would be only . . ."

"Not a few days. A week, maybe."

"What! Doing what?"

"Traveling. I just feel . . ." He lowered his voice. "I just feel I need to sort myself out. Find out what I really want."

"I can't keep the job open indefinitely."

"I know." He didn't say, "I don't want the job." He didn't need to.

Trevor made a short, exasperated noise. "Look, Cal, it's a hard time for you. You should be with people you know, family, not wandering the countryside with that New Age crowd. I presume it's them you're with?"

Cal said nothing.

"I don't see . . . I thought you wanted a good wage, a good life."

"I did," Cal said bleakly. "But that's what took me away from her."

"You couldn't have stayed there forever!" Trevor's voice went soft, irritated. "You mustn't think it was your fault."

"I'll ring again," Cal said. "Don't worry about me. I'm fine." He put the phone down and looked at it a long time.

In the bedroom, he washed his face and turned the TV on, just to hear voices. Then he opened the rucksack and took out his crumpled clothes, his money, and the wrapped package at the bottom.

He laid the two pieces of the broken sword on the bed. They lay on the flowered cover, jagged edges facing each other. He picked them up, and tried to fit them together. They wouldn't meet. With all his strength, he couldn't force them. It was like pushing two like poles of a magnet together; he'd done it in science lessons. An invisible, unbreakable repulsion, and after a second of straining at it the pieces shot to one side, tetchily, refusing. He cut his hand on the sharp blade, and flung it down on the floor in despair.

* Eighteen *

Not one of the retinue knew him.

Peredur

He searched. For a week he tramped the countryside around Ludlow. He bought a pair of cheap hiking boots and photocopied the maps in the library. Every day he went out after breakfast and walked, down valleys with small cold streams rushing over rocks, up in the hills, through miles of frozen fields where curious cows collected around him and followed him in a cloud of breath from stile to stile. After only a day he knew he would never find Corbenic like this, but he couldn't stop; the relief of having something to find, the insistence of the quest calmed him, and the walking, the mindlessness of it, soothed his soul. Out in the fields he could forget about Sutton Street, the funeral, the guilt, he could walk and walk and his mind would be empty, numbed;

only when he trudged back into town at dusk, weary, wet, footsore, did the memories close around him like the old timbered buildings, full of shadows.

His money was running short. He moved to a cheaper bed-and-breakfast, kept by a grumpy couple who seemed to think he was some petty thief; everything was locked up and the room was drab and cold.

Oddly enough, it didn't bother him. The luxuries of Otter's Brook seemed like part of another life that had gone; lying in the damp bed he thought of them and smiled, as he would have at a child with some silly toy. His clothes were getting scruffy. He forgot to wash them. He wasn't eating much. But then he didn't seem to have much appetite.

Once or twice, odd things happened. Coming down the slope of a hill one afternoon, lost in thought, he had looked up and seen, surely, the roof of a castle over the wood below. For a moment it had been there, real and clear, and his heart had surged with some odd bitter joy, but even as he'd stopped and stared it had become clouds, a drifting bank of rain clouds that had tricked him, the battlements and towers breaking up, slowly elongating. The cloud had risen, and had rained on him, a cold, chilling sleet.

Another time, out on the bus from Leominster, he had come down a farm lane, over a stream, and to the edge of a forest, his feet crunching frozen puddles. The forest was dark, coniferous, smelling of sap. Inside it nothing had moved, no bird cheeps, no rustles. Utter stillness.

For a long moment he had stood there on the path, held by the silence. He knew there was something here, something being offered to him, but he was afraid to go in. He had turned back, worked his way around, angry at his own cowardice. Later, in the room, when he had checked the map, no forest had been marked on it at all.

He had not phoned Trevor again.

Sometimes he thought about Hawk and Shadow. Especially Shadow. What had happened to her? Had the police found her? Was she at home? Had she run off again? He had no idea and no way of finding out; he tried not to think of them at all, because that was easier. His mind was full of burned places that he winced away from.

Lying on the bed now, against the hard pillow, hearing the rain pour down the windows outside, he had no idea what to do next. Move on, maybe? South? Down the railway line?

The phone rang, making him jump. He turned his head and stared at it, astonished. It had never rung in the week he'd been here, and no one knew where he was. It had to be the landlord downstairs. Warily, he reached over and picked it up. "Yes."

Silence. A distant, faintly crackling silence. Cal sat up. "Who is this?"

Someone spoke. A whisper. *"Cal?"*

He almost stopped breathing. His heart hurt. Words choked in his mouth.

"Cal. I love you, Cal."

He flung the phone, as if it was hot. It crashed, hard, against the wall, the coiled flex dragging over the little bed-side table; he stared at it in horror.

Outside, the rain pattered on the window. Someone came hurriedly up the stairs and knocked. "All right in there?"

Cal dragged his fingers through his hair. "Yes! Fine."

"Good." Without any asking, the door opened. The land-lord gave a crafty look around, saw the phone. Then his eyes shifted; he was staring, fascinated, at the pieces of the sword. His narrow face darkened. "Staying another week, will you be? The wife wants to know."

"No." Cal was sweating, shaking. For God's sake, couldn't they see he was ill? He had to be ill. He had to be hearing things.

"Leaving then?" the man said, curious. "Sure you're all right?"

"Yes." His teeth were gritted. He wanted to scream.

The old man backed out. "Suit yourself."

Cal barely knew whether he was there or not. When the door had softly shut he crossed to the window with one desperate stride and hauled up the sash, leaning out over the dim alley, breathing in the coldness, letting the rain soak his face and shirt, run down his skin, the shock of it numbing him, till after what seemed like hours the shivering started and wouldn't stop.

Finally he crawled back to bed, pulled the covers over him and lay there, too cold to undress. But he couldn't sleep until he'd got up again and pulled the phone connection out of the wall. Even then, for hours, he lay waiting for it to ring.

There was a castle in Ludlow. He'd already wandered around it, but this morning the old man put the greasy breakfast before him on its chipped plate and said, "Taking that sword of yours down to the reenactment, are you?"

Cal picked up the knife and fork in disbelief. He felt as if his whole life was a circle, bringing him back to things he thought were far behind.

"Reenactment?"

"Sort of siege. For the tourists."

It was no use ignoring it. It couldn't be a coincidence. And someone there might be able to mend the sword.

After breakfast he packed the blade and hilt in a plastic bag, feeling its peculiar shudder in his fingers, and walked down to the castle. Ludlow was different from Chepstow. The castle stood on a cliff, but coming from the town it was level, and the ruins were less stark. There was a round chapel, and the high, broken walls of a great hall.

Outside the gate he paused warily. There it all was. The familiar stalls, the hammering, people in chain mail and long dresses, the horses, the tents. All the things he had come to know.

He watched them for a long time, before he went in. They were not the Company. The banners on the castle were of swans and an eagle, not Arthur's dragon. On the posters outside it said *The Garrison of Salop*. It would be safe.

He wandered around the stalls till he came to a blacksmith; a hot, sweating bald man in a leather apron. Cal took the sword and showed it to him. "Can you fix this?"

The man's huge hands held it reverently. He turned it over, examined the break. Without looking up he said in a broad Geordie brogue, "Where did you get this?"

Irritated, Cal shrugged. "My business. Can you fix it?"

A cold wind whistled around the stalls, clanking a row of hanging daggers one against another.

The blacksmith looked at him steadily. "I don't know. This is a superb blade—or it was. First-class quality. It would take a lot of work; I certainly couldn't do it in one day."

Impatient, Cal shook his head. "How long?"

"A week. In my forge at Hereford."

"How much?" The big question.

The blacksmith weighed the broken pieces in his hands. The sword gleamed in the weak light. He said, "I'm a fool, but thirty quid."

"*Thirty!*"

"That's cheap."

"I haven't got it."

There was a moment of standoff. Finally the blacksmith let out a breath of exasperation. "Okay. I'll do it for twenty-five. Just because I want to work on it, mind you. It's not often I see stuff like this. Agreed?"

Cal nodded, silent. He knew he couldn't afford that either, but it was important that the sword should be whole again.

He took the man's address on a piece of scorched card and turned away, but a woman was waiting behind him, with a clipboard in her hand. She was big too, and wore a Saxon-type dress of some gray coarse fabric, the sleeves pushed well up on her brawny arms. "You a swordsman?" she asked quickly.

Cal shrugged. "I've done some."

"We're a few men short. If you're interested, there's a place for you."

He stopped, still. His first thought was to say no, and then without him knowing, the desire to lose himself, to drown his guilt in some sort of relief was too strong, and he said, "If you want."

"Great. Go up to the tower. Say Janny sent you."

As if he was in some enchantment, Cal climbed the tower stair. He felt it was useless to struggle; that this was meant to happen. Maybe Shadow was here. Maybe the police had blown it, missed her. But even if she was she'd hardly be speaking to him.

The equipment was a mish-mash of helmets and weapons and mail; Kai would have groaned at its lack of authenticity. Cal took a sword and a shield, and some light mail with a silk surcoat over the top.

Then he saw the helmet. It was mail too, and would cover his face except for the narrow sinister slit for his eyes. He put it on.

The reenactment was fun, but slapdash. Not like the Company. For a while he let himself think of nothing but the fighting, and he grew hot and almost happy, slashing with the sword, performing odd choreographed sequences of strokes with total strangers, falling on his knees, the audience on the walls watching and clapping.

As far as he could see the castle was supposed to be besieged, and he was part of the garrison, making a last-ditch defense. He had no idea whether this had ever really happened, or whether he was supposed to be cut down or not, and didn't even care. So when the trumpets rang out and a troop of rescuing knights rode up he was as surprised and pleased as the shrieking kids on the wall.

Until he saw who their leader was.

Instantly he turned and began to struggle back through the crowd; one of the marshals yelled across at him angrily; a blow struck him on the side of the head, so that he staggered.

The knights had dismounted; now they were sweeping

across the field, the weary defenders cheering, the attackers fleeing before them.

Dizzy, Cal climbed to his feet. And faced Hawk. The big man was leaning on his sword, yelling to someone.

Cal said, "Fight with me, stranger."

Hawk turned. He looked at Cal's eyes, muddy and dark. "We're supposed to be on the same side," he said quietly.

"I know," Cal whispered.

"Do I know you?"

"Does that matter?"

Hawk hefted his sword. And swung.

The fight was a good one. The clang of their swords rang out over the remnants of the battlefield; the dead sat up to watch and the exhausted victors drank water from plastic bottles and whistled and cheered.

It was not a fight like he had fought with Kai. That had been real. This was an exhibition, a reveling in the mastery of the blades, the twists and turns, the energy, the total absorption. He knew Hawk could beat him at any moment, but it didn't matter, it was like some dance that they could dance forever, a peace that soothed his soul. It was something like the Grail.

Until a stitch in his side made him gasp and he slid in the mud with a groan and Hawk stood over him, the point of his sword at Cal's neck.

The crowd whooped and roared.

"Let's see who I've beaten," the big man gasped, breathless. He reached down and took the helmet off in one sweep. There was a flash of silence, even in all that racket.

"Cal!" he whispered.

There was no one else in the tower room. Cal eased his aching body onto the floor and sat cross-legged; Hawk brought the can of lager over and a bottle of water. He cracked the can open. "Still off this stuff?"

Cal nodded, drinking the water. Hawk drank too, deep. Neither of them seemed to know what to say; finally Cal asked, "How's everyone? How's Shadow?"

"She's gone."

His heart sank. "Gone? Where?"

"Home." Hawk was eyeing him coldly. "Apparently she was on the run and someone told the police where she was. She said it was you. Was it?"

"Maybe."

"Her parents came. One classy lady, her mother. There was one hell of a row. Arthur was furious; he insisted she went home. Hates deceit, our leader." He drank again. "She never told me no one knew where she was."

For a moment Cal saw his deep hurt. Then Hawk said quietly, "I was sorry to hear about your mother, Cal."

"Forget it." He was harsh; he couldn't even think about that.

Hawk must have noticed. "What are you doing here, laddie?"

"Looking. For Corbenic."

The big man came and sat down. Then he said, "Not only you. Since that night at Caerleon the whole Company have made a vow to quest for the Grail. Arthur has sent us all out; we're looking for you, and for this Corbenic. Though when someone told the Hermit he laughed so crazily he scared us all."

"Looking for me?"

"Yes. So is your uncle, I hear. He's been onto the police; they found out you weren't in Bangor."

Cal felt cold, and furious. "He has no right!"

"He's worried. So were we all." Hawk drank the dregs of the can and put it carefully on the shaven boards of the floor. "Cal, I'm going to tell you about something that happened to me, years ago. I was out riding, and it was late, dark, and I got lost. I came to this place. Marshy. Birds flying out of the reeds. There was a sort of causeway, a creaky wicker track, and I rode across it. Trees met overhead. A really eerie place; I had to bend down and look ahead, and there was some sort of light at the end."

He paused, staring at the beer can. Outside the clatter of hooves came up from the courtyard. Tense, Cal waited. "It was too dark to make the place out. The horse was nervous; I had to dismount, and I never found the light. There seemed to be some sort of great hall, and when I opened the door and went in it was full of people, and there was a feast going on. The odd thing was they were all really glad to see me; there was a fire and dry clothes all ready, but then I turned round and they saw my face. They looked devastated. "This isn't the one," they said. They were whispering. "'*This isn't the one.*'" He picked the can up, drinking the last drips.

"What happened?"

"It all vanished, laddie."

"Vanished?"

Hawk looked at him. "Lady Shadow, God bless her, never quite believed your story. But I did, son. Because I think I've been to that castle too, and failed, maybe worse than you. Maybe a lot of us have been there." After a moment he said, "Come back with me, Cal. You shouldn't be alone. Not now."

Cal put his head in both palms. "I have to find the Grail, Hawk, I have to."

"Then let me come with you."

"I can't."

"Why not? It'll be easier with someone else."

That was true. For a moment he hesitated; then stood up and pulled the dented mail off, and stacked the borrowed sword on its rack. "All right. I'll get my stuff and meet you back here. Say, an hour."

But Hawk said softly, "Don't lie to me, laddie."

Halfway through the door Cal stopped. The big man was watching him. He tried to smile. "Sorry," he whispered. "It's

just . . . in the story Percival has to go back on his own. I have
to do this, Hawk."

For a moment he thought Hawk would grab him, force
him to come. But the big man began unlacing his armor
grimly. "I'll wait for the hour," he said.

The bed-and-breakfast was in a narrow street of half-
timbered houses that leaned their heads together above the
pavements. By the time he got to the corner it was late afternoon and the sky was heavy with sullen yellow clouds. Flakes
of snow, small and hard, had begun to fall.

The osprey was perched on the railings of the churchyard.

Cal stopped dead, and it shrieked at him, one sharp
screech of warning. Then it rose and flew to the top of the
pinnacled tower, staring down.

Cautiously, Cal peered down the lane. There was a police
car outside the bed-and-breakfast. The old couple were at the
door, talking to an officer. Eagerly. Nosily.

Cal pulled his head back and swore viciously. How could
they have found him? Trevor, yes, but how here?

Then he remembered taking money out of his account
yesterday with the cashpoint card at the machine in the High
Street. That was it. They could trace that. He felt like a crim-
inal, like someone hunted. It infuriated him.

Quickly, barely thinking, he went back and up the alley,
slipped in through the kitchen door and ran upstairs. Hurriedly

he gathered his clothes, soap, maps, shoes, jamming them in the rucksack. Then he ran down and was out before the old man had finished his sentence.

All the way through the darkening streets of the town he ran, the snow falling on him and the osprey high overhead, swooping between the rooftops.

At the blacksmith's stall he found only a small boy; pushing him aside he grabbed the sword in its plastic bag. It gave him a sly dig of pain under one nail.

The kid sputtered through a mouthful of crisps. "Hey! You can't take that! My dad . . ."

"Tell your dad I've changed my mind."

It was getting dark as he came around to the gate. The stalls were closing; snow lay on their awnings. Horses were being led out to vans, a warm, snuffling parade, steam rising from them. Somewhere in the castle Hawk was waiting for him. He turned away and walked into the falling snow.

* Nineteen *

Everywhere he went he found the streets waste and the houses in ruins.

Conte du Graal

"T his do?" The truck driver braked.

"Oh . . . Yes. Thanks." Jolted out of a half sleep, Cal opened his eyes and hastily grabbed his bag. They were in a busy street, packed with people.

"It's Market Day," the driver said, changing gear. "Can't stop."

"Right. Thanks again."

Cal scrambled awkwardly out of the cab and stood back in the doorway of an empty shop, while the truck wheezed and hooted its way down the congested street.

People were everywhere. They walked in the road, chatted, waved. There were young girls dressed in fashionable clothes, old couples, boys on skateboards, farmers in a uniform of dark green worn coats and caps. This was Abergavenny. He'd never been here before.

He picked up his bag wearily and slung it over one shoulder, and pushed along the pavement. The pressure of the crowd, its laughter and life, was warm; it caught him up and swept him into the market, and he wandered aimlessly among the bleating of sheep and the stalls, looking at antiques and old amber jewelry and books and china.

He was so tired. Last night he had tried to sleep in a small hotel in Hereford, but something had been tapping on the window all night; it had woken him from broken dreams, and he had got up with a groan and staggered over. When he'd pulled back the curtains the osprey had been there.

It wouldn't fly away. All night it had shuffled and roosted on the windowsill; he had lain awake watching it, its yellow eyes open as if it slept like that, fixing him with fierce, unblinking scrutiny. Accusing him. Even when he had drawn the curtains again and turned his back on it he had felt that gaze, tried to shrink from it, hide under the blankets. But it was still there, like the hatred he had for himself.

Then he had thought, if the bird was here, surely Corbenic must be near.

Now, in the noisy, echoing racket of the street, he rubbed his face and longed for some coffee. What the hell was wrong with him? He'd give this up. He'd go back, right now, to Chepstow, and to the neat black-and-white bedroom at

Trevor's; he'd wear his suit and go to the office and to hell with them all, and their crazy disappearing castles. He'd dump the sword. He'd do that right now.

He took it out, still in its plastic bag and thrust it blindly into a bin on the street and marched away; before he'd taken three steps a shriek of pain skewered him from behind.

A little girl was standing by the bin and screaming. Her mother ran up, and swung the girl up in terror. "What's the matter, darling?"

"It bit me." The child wailed, holding out a cut finger.

"What did?"

"It! That man left it there."

The woman grabbed the bag, opened it and stared in disbelief. Then she looked up and eyed Cal. He wanted to run but couldn't. Passersby flowed around him, turning curiously.

"What a stupid place to put something that sharp!" Furious, she flung it down on the pavement, a metallic crash.

With great control, tense in every muscle, Cal bent and picked the bag up. He turned and walked away, hearing every syllable of the woman's comforting of the child stab him like a knife in the back.

"I'll dump you so deep in the river," he murmured, "you'll never, ever trouble me again."

The sword settled in its bag smugly.

At the cashpoint he put his card in, glancing quickly around in case anyone was watching. He punched the numbers; the machine made a small chuntering noise. Then, with shocking finality, it swallowed his card.

Aghast, Cal stared. A stark, printed message came up on the screen. THIS CARD IS WITHHELD. PLEASE CONTACT YOUR BRANCH FOR FURTHER INFORMATION.

For an instant the implications didn't hit him; when they did he turned and ran, down the street, around the corner, up a steep ramp into what seemed like a park, checking at every turn no one was following, sprinting up a flight of steps between wintry ruined flowerbeds and collapsing onto a park bench.

Trevor had stopped his card. Furious, he ground his hands into fists and then thought, no, maybe not. Maybe he had just run out of money. In either case, the result was the same.

He searched his pockets, dug out his wallet from the rucksack, gathered coins and notes. Fifteen pounds forty-two pence. Not enough for another night's stay anywhere. Maybe enough for the train fare home. All his money gone and nothing to show for it! He thought of how he had once gloated over the bank statements. How he had felt so good about that.

He put the money in his pocket and sat back, looking down on the flat, waterlogged river meadows that stretched out below him, their flooded paths iced to shining deathtraps where kids slid and screeched, tiny voices rising to him.

He would not go to Otter's Brook.

He shivered, the cold wind cutting him. He had sworn he would find the Grail and he would find it. The osprey was here. The castle must be close. He got up and wandered along the path, thinking hard. He'd have to watch every penny. Eat carefully. Chips. Anything cheap. And sleep out. In January! The thought of that was appalling but he made himself face it. That was where he was going wrong. To find Corbenic he would have to give up everything, to walk right out of the world of towns and bed-and-breakfasts. To do what he had sometimes dreamed of sleepily on long train journeys, to walk into the greenwood and not come back.

Wherever it was it was near, and far. Like Bron had been. Like his mother had been.

The park curled around a castle. He stared up at the gray walls in dull, wry appreciation, not even surprised anymore. This whole borderland was a line of castles; they were passing him from one to the next, but none of them was the right one.

He took a buttered roll from his bag and ate it; it was hard and crusty, left over from breakfast, but it was all he was allowing himself for now.

Under it, still wrapped in its box and tissue paper, was the pale gray tie. Cal brought it out and opened it on his knee. The tie was beautiful. Its silk shone. It smelled of Thérèse's expensive perfume. It was all the things he had ever desired, all the comfort and elegance and taste. For a long moment he let himself enjoy it, remembering the pleasure of buying it. Then he folded it up, his hands shaking with cold. He still had the receipt, and there was a branch of the shop just around the corner. It was one way to get some money.

With the cash he bought cheap fruit in the market, and water, and matches and looked at the sleeping bags in the hiking shop, but they were too expensive. By the time he walked out of the town on a back lane that led up past farms and under the railway line into the countryside, it was past three and already getting dark. The osprey swooped overhead, a shadow in the growing twilight. Then it flew off to the west, and was gone.

A mile or so down the lane he came to a stile on his right; above it a leaning metal post pointed. PUBLIC FOOTPATH, it said, in Welsh and English. Beyond it a scrubby ungrazed field stretched down to a small wood. Nothing moved in its stillness; no birds sang, there were no cattle or sheep. In the dim twilight over the trees a few faint stars shone.

Cal climbed the gate, and entered the Waste Land.

* Twenty *

"If thou go there, thou wilt not come back alive."
"Wilt thou be a guide to me there?" asked Peredur.
"I will show thee a way," said she.

Peredur

She was screaming at him. It happened; usually she was tearful and slurred her speech, but sometimes, without warning, she was screaming. Only now it was in some other language, French maybe, and he couldn't understand it. They were in Trevor's immaculate room, and she snatched up the Greek vase from the glass table and threw it; it smashed in pieces against the pale walls.

Cal said, "Look. It's all right. It doesn't matter." It was what he always said. Soothing noises. Anything.

He couldn't remember how the row had started. But it was his fault. He knew that.

She flung a glass at him; he ducked and Guinness spattered the wall. He stared at it in horror. Now she was throwing cushions, and an ashtray, and the radio, which crashed into the glass shelves and brought the whole lot down on top of him, a showering of light fragments, cold, cutting.

She was screaming in his ears, close to his face.

He opened his eyes.

The wind. It was the wind, howling, and it was snow that was falling on him; snow that had drifted in a great scatter from the laden branches of the hedge. He groaned, wormed farther in, sweating despite the raw weather. He didn't want to wake, because that meant the cold came back, the terrible ache in his fingers, the numbness of his face, the shivering. But if he slept even for a moment he dreamed, and the dreams were worse, they were a torment, and there was no way away from them.

Curled, he closed his eyes tight, feeling the tiny rustle of dried leaves against his cheek, the icy mud soft and yielding, the infinitesimal patter of snow. All across the fields it was falling, tiny hard flakes, and it was settling and not melting, and since late that afternoon the land had been turning white. Only the trees were dark; stark leafless shapes.

It was his third night in the dark land. Or third week? For a moment he couldn't remember and snapped his eyes open in alarm, staring at the black thorns and briars above him.

He had been walking so long his body ached and his legs felt trembly; he had been hungry days ago but that had gone now, leaving a sort of light-headed emptiness. The food had more or less run out; he had some hazelnuts and rock-hard cheese but those had to be kept. Supplies. He grinned, weakly. Like the games he had played years back, with the other kids in the park. Survival. Camouflage.

Snow drifted into his eyes. He closed them again, and the darkness seemed warmer.

Shadow and Hawk were pulling him into the van. It was a long way up, there were too many steps, and over the door was a sign saying VACANCIES. It made him laugh; he couldn't stop. Weakly he giggled, and Shadow snapped, "What? What's so funny?" But before he could tell her, the microwave pinged, and Hawk went to it.

"No!" Cal jumped up out of the warm chair. "Don't open that!"

Slowly, with a deliberate grin, Hawk opened it. Fish poured out, a shining, slithering, stinking mass. They cascaded out, onto the floor, filling the van up, more and more of them, and Leo flung his net out and Bron sat in the boat and said, "One day, we may catch a real treasure, a fish with a ring in its belly. Like the old tales."

Cal sat up, pushing the fish away, and his hands were cold and the icy mush plopped and slid. He was on a slab in a market stall. He was under the hedge. He was freezing.

Get up. Get up and walk. You had to. If you didn't you'd go to sleep and never wake up, all the books told you that. Find shelter. Light a fire.

He staggered up, scratching his face on the brambles. The rucksack was light; he barely felt it now as he flung it on and climbed out of the ditch. At once the wind struck him. He bent, wrapping his arms around his body, clutching his thin coat tight, struggling over the humped, tussocky, boggy field. There had to be a road, a way back.

But he had been looking forever. It was as if he had entered some other world. This was not Wales. This was not England. He had fallen into the crack between them. He had walked off the map. There were no birds and no houses. In the night no lights shone, not even the distant red glimmer of town streetlights reflecting on cloud. He had walked on and on in a landscape of overgrown meadows and desolate hillsides, of small, cascading streams, bitter cold to drink from, tasting of ice. Long ago he had told himself he was a fool, and had tried to head back to the road, but there was no road, anywhere, anymore, and none of the maps were any use because this place was not real anyway. He had burned them, crouching in a small copse, holding his swollen fingers over the useless yellow flames.

Once a knight had jumped out from under a stone, and fought him. He had the bruises. He knew it had happened.

And now there were these sheep. A field of them, white

sheep, and then a river, narrow and stony, and beyond it a field sloping, and the sheep in that were all black. As he stumbled down the frozen slope he saw a white ewe cross the stream, slithering in and splashing across. It came out, and it was black. It cropped the grass. He stopped dead, watching. After a while a black sheep came this way. It came out of the water white. His eyes had been on it all the time. He hadn't seen when it changed.

Taking a drink from the plastic water bottle, he rubbed a hand down his stubbly face and walked on. His lips felt cracked; his skin raw with the frost. As he walked among them the sheep moved apart, watching, chewing solidly, and at the stream he knelt and fearfully touched the surface with his finger. The rocky bed had a reddish tinge. Weeds hung under it.

He stood up, and waded across.

Did he change? He was colder, certainly; he shivered, his feet were soaked, and there were holes in the cheap boots that he hadn't noticed before.

The land had changed though, it was steeper and rockier, and there were mountains now; it was darker. Time had passed. Where had it gone?

And a tree on the bank of a different river was burning, root to tip, half in leaf and half in flames, and as he backed around its trunk the heat of it scorched him, and on the leafy side birds sang, unsinged.

The sky darkened, lit, darkened. Moon and stars flashed over him; the sun circled like a hidden eye, watching.

He was wandering in his own delirium, his own nightmares. Sometimes he didn't know if he walked awake or asleep; people opened secret doors in his head and came out and were trudging with him; Kai once, and the Grail girl, wrapped in a green brocade cloak, nagging at him. And behind him, always, so that he didn't even have to turn and check she was there anymore, walked his mother, her hair with strange blond highlights that didn't suit her, her clothes new, a red skirt, a gray sweater, and no mud on her, and no snow.

She pursued him; stumbling on the furrows, he knew she was there and said, "Leave me alone."

But she only answered what she always answered, a whisper that was almost a threat. *"I love you, Cal."*

He tripped and fell, full length in the dark, a jarring thud. Breathless, he lay there. He wouldn't get up. He couldn't. His eyes were blind with water, hot tears that swelled from somewhere deep; he sobbed silently, then aloud, a yell of anguish.

"Bron!" he screamed. "I'm here! I'm looking for you! I can't do anymore."

Silence. Only the hiss of snow. And far off, the faint creaking of burdened trees, an eerie, terrible sound.

Cal pulled himself up on knees and elbows, a convulsion of despair. *"For God's sake show me the way out!"*

The reply came from behind him. With a gasp he whipped around, saw the glimmer of it move down the hedgerow. An animal. Big. Four legs. He scrambled up. It was hard to see, in the driving snow. White. A deer. A dog?

Floundering, he dragged his feet out of the mud and went after it, crazily swaying, because it would have shelter, it might be a farm dog, there might be a lighted window and a door that would open for it, a voice, calling out, a fire.

Snow drifted in his face. Wiping it away he slid and hurried down the rough grass slope, the blur of white far in front, and as it jumped the ditch into the copse down there he was sure it was a sheep, but when he reached the frozen reeds and crunched over them, lurching on the tilted slabs, he caught sight of it again, a narrow face, and it was slimmer, a white deer. It turned and entered the wood. With barely a hesitation, he went after it.

Usually, he avoided woods. They were too silent. You never knew what might be lurking in them. But now he went straight on, ducking under the low outer branches of pliant hazel, the snow dusting down on his head and shoulders. It was dark. There was no wind in here. Ahead, lost in shadows, the animal rustled.

He had to fight his way through, thorns snagging him and briars whipping back to scratch his face, and he was sure, suddenly and joyfully, that he was in the right place. The garden at Corbenic had been like this; he'd had to fight his way out, and that strange, childish idea came back to him of the castle in the fairy tale, hidden behind its tangle of growth.

His foot slipped; he reached out to steady himself. He caught hold of something slim and tall, a pole. As his hand came away it was wet and sticky with some dark mess; he jerked back, hissing with terror, rubbing his palm frantically on his sleeve, because into his mind with lightning clarity had come the image of the spear that bled. Then, carefully, he looked closer. It was a broken fence. Long ruined. Bending, he scraped through.

On the other side, a green mass rose up in front of him: ivy-covered walls, ghostly now with a phosphorescence of snow, ruinous and shapeless.

Just at his right, a small panting sound. In the dark, his fingers stretched out, groping, searching; he almost dreaded what he would touch, but when he found it it was a familiar shock, the slightly greasy wet fur, the lick of a hot rough tongue. A dog.

The dog did not bark, or whimper. It moved, padding and snuffling its way through the undergrowth, and Cal went with it, whispering, "Wait. Wait, boy," terrified that it would leave him.

Under the walls of the building they went, a progression of rustles, and when Cal paused and hissed, "Where are you?" the night was silent. But not dark.

Light was coming from somewhere above him; he looked

up and saw the moon, the frostiest of crescents, caught in a sudden gap of cloud, and the moon shone on an image that seemed to hang in the black and silver of the walls, an image of a golden cup, held in two hands.

For a second it was there. Then the cloud fragmented; the darkness was a window, its stained glass broken, a patchwork of vacancies and facets of ice, seated figures, a shattered supper.

This was not Corbenic. It was some sort of chapel.

Cal crouched by the wall, his breath a cloud. He was ill with disappointment; it overwhelmed him like the blackness over the moon. It darkened his whole mind.

The rough tongue licked his hand.

The thought came, out of what seemed a deep well of pain, that at least there might be a roof, some shelter, so he stood and groped for a doorway, found a pointed arch swathed thick with ivy and bindweed and stinging nettles and holly.

Ducking under, he saw the chapel was a green bower of growth. It stank of damp and mildew and mold. Weeds had climbed all over it, sprouted and tangled; the roof was a web of snow-littered branches. And under them, in the farthest corner, a fire was crackling.

The dog crossed a slant of moonlight, a slither of darkness. It nosed and snuffled a huddle of shadow. And the shadow raised its head and said, "So I haven't left my moulting cage in vain."

✳ Twenty-one ✳

If you had seen all I have seen you would not sleep.

Oianau of Merlin

Cal stepped inside warily. A handful of kindling was thrown on the fire; the flames spat a sudden crackle of sparks up into the ruined roof.

The Hermit sat cross-legged, his patchwork coat spread around him, leaning on a large bundle at his back. His narrow, crazy eyes glinted red in the flickering light. Behind him the dog went and lay down with a faint sigh, chin on paws.

Cal came and sat by the fire. The warmth of it was such a relief that for a long moment he simply absorbed it, as if something deep in him was frozen hard and had to be thawed. When he managed to speak his voice was rusty with disuse, his throat dry and hoarse. "I suppose I should have known it would be you."

Merlin grinned, and fished in a filthy knapsack at his side. He threw something over; Cal caught it and found it was bread, still slightly soft. He tore a bit off and chewed it.

"Did I not prophesy, wise fool, that we should meet here where all but shame has deserted you?" The man's voice was a whisper; Cal knew he was mad, probably dangerous. He didn't care. Stretching his weary legs out he said, "Have you got anything to drink?"

A bottle. And then, to his worn surprise, a cup. Merlin poured carefully, his black and broken fingernails poking through torn mittens. He held the cup out.

"What is it?" It smelled of berries.

"Something of my own. It will make you sleep."

Forever, Cal thought, but he was too thirsty and he drank, and the taste was a deep red taste and sweet. As he put the cup down he felt a drowsy warmth flood his head and chest. There had been alcohol in it.

Merlin leaned back on the patient dog. "You have walked a long time in the Waste Land."

"Three days."

"If you say so." He spat into the flames. "Maybe much longer. Maybe years. You have not found what you seek."

It wasn't a question. Suddenly Cal felt the tension of the dark land drain away from him; though it was only just out there, through that ivy-grown arch, he felt as if he had some-how come to somewhere else. His mind cleared. He leaned forward. "Listen. At Caerleon. The . . . girl, woman, what-ever, said I hadn't been able to ask about the Grail because of my mother. I left her. Did you know that?"

Merlin watched, unmoving.

"I just walked out on her. I hated her. I was ashamed of her. But I can't do anything about that now, because she's dead, she took an overdose." He clenched his hands together. "Don't you see, I can't do anything about it! It's too late. It'll always be too late now. Forever." His words were breaking apart.

Slowly, Merlin stirred the fire. When he spoke his voice was sad. "She follows you."

Cal looked up. "What?"

"Like a shadow. She is your shadow. She's a dog at your heels, I know, I have my own doom at mine. You wish it to be too late, but it is not. It never is."

"I hate her."

Merlin laughed, tossing the stick down. "Not so. You have forgotten how to love. That's a different sorrow."

Behind him, tiny leaves were sprouting on the ivy. Cal watched them, distracted. "I can't forgive her."

"And does she forgive you?"

"I don't . . ."

"You do. You must turn around and ask her."

Cal stared in blank fear. Then the Hermit laughed, a dry, brittle laugh that made the dog's ears prick uneasily.

"How?" Cal whispered.

Merlin leaned forward, eyes bright. "You have already drunk the means."

The chapel was a green gloom. It was closing on them, the ivy growing, unfurling, climbing with small crisp rustles over the walls and along the floor, curling fronds around the dog's belly. It was growing from Merlin, from his hair and beard, his fingernails; he was a green man, made of leaves and stems and bines, they were raveling out and tangling around Cal, stopping him breathing. He felt the stems cover him, warm him; he snuggled into them.

Behold the marvels, they whispered. *Behold the mysteries of the Grail.*

But all he saw was Sutton Street. It was his old bedroom, with the stained carpet and the frowsty bed and the thud of next door's stereo through the walls. He lay there in his old T-shirt and pajama trousers, and Shadow was sitting on the floor next to the radiator that leaked.

She glared up at him. "You! You've got a nerve!"

He sat up, stared around, confused. "It shouldn't be you . . ."

"Why the hell not!" She was blazing with anger. "Who asked you to interfere, Cal! It was none of your business, none of it!"

"I thought . . ."

"I was happy with the Company! Now look what you've done to me! Look where I am!" She scrambled up, and she was strange to him, as if her shape had shifted, her face washed and unveiled and unfamiliar. She grabbed hold of his wrist, sharp nails digging in. "The police came! My mother—oh, you should have heard her. She should have won ten Oscars for that performance."

He was hurting. She was hurting him. "I thought . . . It's just you had everything I ever wanted. And you ran away from it."

"Money's not happiness." She dropped his wrist and stepped back. "Private schools and a big house and three cars, that's not happiness. Didn't you ever think I could be unhappy too?"

He shook his head, numbed. He couldn't believe that. He still couldn't.

The stereo thumped. He got off the bed and sat on its edge, leaning over and running his hands through his hair as he'd used to, when it had woken him, when he'd been waiting for his mother to get home.

Shadow watched him, rigid a moment. Then she came and sat next to him.

The light from the lamppost outside flickered and went out. In the darkness she said, "I hate it here, Cal. I'm all on my own. Find me."

The voice wasn't hers. It came from the woman sitting by the cauldron who looked up as he sat, pushing aside the tangle of nightshade and hemlock.

This was a dark place. A cave, maybe, an underworld. On the red walls he saw the old graffiti from Sutton Street, and smudgy paintings of animals, and handmarks.

She shuffled up to make room for him. "I've been waiting, Cal."

The cauldron was huge. Bronze, dented, with a curling red enamel pattern around the rim. It hung from three great chains that rose up into the darkness and vanished, as if they reached to the sky. In it, liquid bubbled and plopped. Steam rose, half hiding his mother.

It was she who wore the tattoos now, not a web like Shadow, but blue lines on her cheeks. She took his hand, and stroked it. "Did you think it was an accident?" she said quietly.

"I don't know. Was it?"

She didn't answer. Then she said, "All our lives, minute by minute, lead to what we are." She looked around and laughed, that rare silvery laugh he had not heard for years. "I used to be scared of the dark. But this isn't so bad. Not with a few decent curtains."

He tried to smile. Steam blurred between them. "Do you forgive me?" he whispered.

The cauldron bubbled. When he knew she was not there, was not going to answer, he stood and looked into it, and saw that fish swam in there, shoals of them, though the liquid was red. One of the fish leaped; he jerked back as it flashed out and back, barely missing his face with its tail. And three drops of the blood fell out onto the snow. He stared at them, because they were the heart of it, the secret, melting into each other, pitting the white frosted crystals.

"Cal."

Owein. One of the Company. He caught Cal's arm but Cal flung him off. "Leave me alone."

There were feathers now, black, from a bird's wing. Black. White. Red.

The Company were here, all around him. "Leave him to me," Kai was saying; he came over. "Arthur wants you. We've been looking for you."

"Leave me ALONE!" He had the sword, he struck out with it, and Kai's parry was hurried and wrong, and Cal stepped in close and hurled the man back, so that he landed sprawling, the dark expensive coat in the slush, his fair hair in his eyes. Astonished, he stared up. Cal laughed, then turned, threatening. "That goes for all of you!"

Darkness. Light. Blood. These were what the Grail held. There was a great truth, a breathtaking secret and he almost had hold of it, a door he had almost tugged open, the handle smooth under his fingers, the castle walls rising in front of him, and this was Corbenic and he was home, and a voice said, "Even me, Cal?" and it all vanished and he turned, white with fury.

But Hawk was unarmed. "Wake up, laddie," he whispered.

✳ ✳ ✳

He was warmer. Green light was filtering through leaves onto his face, and the dog was snoring beside him, a comfortable lump curled around his legs. Stiff, Cal sat up.

The fire smoldered smokily. Birds were singing, and the sun glinted through the overgrown windows of the chapel. Of Merlin there was no sign.

Pushing the sleepy dog off he climbed up and brushed leaf dust and soil and grime from his ruined jeans and jacket, rubbed his stubbly face and yawned. He needed a wash and a drink.

Outside, ducking under the archway, he found a small spring that bubbled out of the rocks, a tiny, crystal-clear water source that he drank from again and again, splashing the icy drops on his face and hands, down his neck, as if he could never have enough of it.

As he dried himself awkwardly with his sleeve, he listened to the trickle and splash of the water. It was loud. It hadn't been there last night. He looked around.

The chapel was tilted, as if some great blow had struck it. Its walls were nearly smothered, but he could see carved stones worn almost to smoothness by centuries of rain; coming up to one he pushed the ivy aside and felt with his fingers the gnarled grotesque faces, the cavalcade of knights that curved around the pillar. Small grains dislodged and fell from under his fingertips.

"Breakfast," Merlin said cheerfully.

Cal spun.

The Hermit leaned against a tree. He waved a hand over a spread of leaves and nuts, daintily arranged.

Cal came and sat down. He looked at the unappetizing mess. "Thanks."

Merlin selected an ancient hazelnut with great care. To Cal's amazement, when he spoke he sounded completely normal. "There are lots of old stories about the Grail. Some say it was a Celtic cauldron. Others the cup of the Last Supper. There are different versions of the myth, but the most well known has Joseph of Arimathea bringing the cup to Britain, and possibly to the Island of Avalon."

Cal said, "Where's that?"

"Beyond. *Where falls not hail, or rain, or any snow, nor ever wind blows loudly. Where I will heal me of my grievous wound.'* Some say Glastonbury."

Cal had heard of it. "There's a rock festival there."

"Indeed." Merlin scratched his tangle of hair with long fingers.

"You think I should look there? For Corbenic?"

The Hermit smiled. "That is within you. You might find that anywhere. Percival fails to ask about the Grail and must return to the castle. That was always your mistake, not going back. But first . . ."

"First I have something else to do. Someone else to see."

Merlin's eyes slid to the woods. "Your shadow."

Wary, Cal stood. "Maybe. But first, how do I get out of this place?"

"You just wish to be out." Merlin picked up a nut and tossed it away; it hit the dog. He turned and glared at her. "You! Bitch!" He scrambled up hastily, swung to Cal. "How long has she been here? Has she heard everything? Has she found the secrets yet, the secrets of my power?"

His heart sinking, Cal took a step back. He went into the chapel and found his bag, and filled his water bottle hastily at the tiny spring.

Merlin was still cursing the dog. His face was narrow; he had spread his hands and was muttering things about pigs and apple trees and a prison under a stone. He was crazy. He should be in some hospital. Cal watched him in silence.

Suddenly Merlin's eyes went to Cal, sly. "The knight has spent his vigil in the chapel. The knight continues the quest."

Cal nodded. Then he turned and walked away. Deep in the wood he turned and looked back. Merlin and the dog were eyeing each other warily. Then the dog yawned and lay down.

Cal walked for twenty minutes before he found the lane. Climbing over a stile he scrambled down into it, a deep lane between two hedges, sparse now with winter twigs. Turning to his right, he followed it. It led downhill, around a bend, widened out, became a two-lane road, rose into a bridge.

CORBENIC

He leaned on the bridge rail in a bewilderment of noise. Below him, in a thundering explosion of trucks and fast cars and searing speed, a motorway stretched in both directions. As far as his eyes could see.

✳ Twenty-two ✳

He emerged from the forest and came upon a most wondrous land.

2nd Continuation

Bath was beautiful. He wandered around its shops in weary appreciation, looking in at the fabulous furniture, the sumptuous giftware. Swaths of expensive fabric and chandeliers hung in shop windows; there were open-topped buses with Japanese tourists and taped commentaries about the Romans, Jane Austen, John Wood. And the streets amazed him—they were so grand, so sweeping, elegant facades of golden stone. Classy. That Shadow lived here impressed him.

He had to ask a few times for Great Pulteney Street; it was over a quaint bridge with tiny shops on each side. When he'd crossed it he stared down the wide expanse of perfectly matching elegant houses. Each one was Georgian, with a big painted front door, the steps in front leading down into an area behind black railings, where the servants would once have lived.

At Shadow's number he stopped. There were window boxes with tiny daffodils and primulas, yellow and blue. The door was a glossy red, the huge brass handle gleaming, the curtains looped back. It all screamed money.

He swallowed. He'd caught sight of his reflection briefly in a window in town and had been shocked. He looked ten years older. His hair was matted and his clothes filthy with mud and dirt; he must stink. Merlin had loaned him an old army coat that came down past his knees, tattered khaki but warmer than just his jacket. He looked down at it with a sour smile. A few weeks ago he wouldn't have touched it with a barge pole. But that was a lifetime away. He climbed the steps and rang the bell, turning and watching the street warily.

"Yes?" The tone was distasteful. He turned back and saw a woman of about fifty, stocky, in a flower-print dress. Her sleeves were rolled up, her hands floury. It wasn't what he'd expected.

"Hi. I'm a friend of Sh . . . Sophie. Is it possible to speak to her?"

The woman looked him up and down. "She's at school. Who shall I say called?"

"Cal," he began, "but . . ." The door shut in his face. "Bloody snob," he snarled. But he wasn't surprised.

It was two o'clock, and fairly warm. He walked back to the bridge and down some steps at the side and along the river-bank, then sat and watched the water thunder over the weir.

There were two swans on the river, performing an elegant bobbing and intertwining love dance; joggers and tourists stopped to watch them.

Cal lay down on the bench and dozed in the weak sun. If she wouldn't help him, he didn't know what he'd do. The money was gone. He wouldn't sit in an underpass and beg. Glastonbury, Merlin had said. On the maps he'd looked at in the bookshops it wasn't so far. Perhaps he could walk there. But he needed food.

He must have slept. Faces and voices disturbed him, as they always did. His mother said, "Get yourself something from the chippie for your tea," and he laughed sourly and said, "What's new," and then sat up, cold and strained, because she was dead.

She was dead.

He still couldn't take that in. He knew it, understood it, couldn't bear it, was glad of it. And yet she was here, still a weight on him. He got up quickly and went back up to the street.

After twenty minutes leaning in a doorway, he saw Shadow coming along. She looked so different. Her hair was lighter, and she wore the school uniform he'd seen in the photo on the poster, a blue blazer, a tartan skirt. And the tattoo was gone. There was another girl with her, dressed the same. They had a magazine open and were looking at it, laughing.

His heart thudded. She didn't look unhappy. For a moment he froze. He couldn't speak to her. He should go away and leave her. And then, with an almost desperate lunge, he made himself step out right in front of them. "Shadow," he said.

The friend gave a small scream. Startled, Shadow looked up. Her face was a blank shock. Then she said, "Cal?"

He tried to smile. Passersby turned. In a flash he saw what they saw: a homeless good-for-nothing harassing two well-heeled girls. Until Shadow grabbed his arm. "What are you doing here? *What's happened to you?*"

Stupidly, stupidly, he felt his voice choke. He shook his head. He knew if he answered he'd break down.

She moved fast. She said something to the friend, ushered Cal firmly up the steps and opened the door with a key. Then he was inside, the door closing behind him, with one last glimpse of the girl on the pavement clutching her magazine in astonished surprise.

The hall was huge, carpeted, mirrored. She led him into a big room at the back and sat him on the sofa. He felt weak, and useless.

"Shadow, I'm so sorry," he whispered.

She crouched. "Not now, Cal. Look at the state of you! How long since you've eaten?"

He couldn't remember.

She went out. In front of him the fire roared over fake

coals, but the heat was real and he was glad of it. He took one quick look round. Chippendale furniture. Portraits, great gilt framed things. Real. A clock like something out of *The Antiques Road Show*. He felt small, shriveled up.

Shadow came back, and the woman was with her, carrying a tray, silver, with a teapot on it and small cakes. The woman stared at him with dislike.

"This is Marj," Shadow said quickly. "She works for us. Put it down there, and go and run him a bath, will you? Are there any clothes that would fit him?"

Their low voices discussed him as if he wasn't there. Maybe he wasn't. He felt so light-headed and weak he wasn't even sure.

Then Shadow was giving him tea and he was drinking it. The hot liquid shocked him into awareness; for a second it made him think of the time in Hawk's van after the fight in the Dell; maybe Shadow thought of it too, because she said, "We've all been so worried about you!"

He smiled, trying to eat some cake. It tasted like ashes. He needed to explain but she wouldn't let him talk and he was glad, because the words would have come out all jumbled and useless. While she fussed around upstairs he laid his head back on the plush sofa, and if he had closed his eyes he would have slept.

Then she was saying, "Cal. Come on."

* * *

The bathroom was white and gold. He sat on a chair and looked at it. "Wow. Beats the van."

Shadow grinned, preoccupied. "There are towels, and some old clothes of my father's. They'll be big but you're as tall as him. Come down when you're ready."

As she went out he said, "I didn't think you'd be speaking to me."

She looked at him hard. "Why not? It seems we're both liars."

The hot water was such luxury he could not believe his own luck. Drowsing in it he felt the aches of his body gradually ease; there were cuts and stings and bruises he had no idea that he had, and he couldn't remember where they had come from. The whole of the time in the Waste Land seemed far off, the green chapel like a dream. And yet Merlin's ragged coat hung over the chair.

He soaped and rinsed and scraped himself till it hurt. Then he looked in the mirror. His face was strange to him, hollow-eyed, thin, stubbled. He had lost weight; he couldn't understand how much. He dressed in the jeans, and shirt. They were so baggy at the waist he had to use his old belt to keep them up, but they felt crisp and clean, and expensive. Rather than pull his mucky boots on he went downstairs in just the socks.

Shadow was putting the phone down. She turned. "That's better!"

"Who were you ringing?" His voice was tense, paranoid.

"Trevor."

"Shadow, you . . ."

"Oh Cal, for heaven's sake! He's been worried sick about you! Last month he was here begging me to help him."

"Last month?" He stared at her. At the primulas behind her, through the window. The swans, he thought. The warm weather. *How long had he been in the Waste Land?* He sat down unsteadily. "What date is it?"

"The third."

"Of?"

She came over, concerned. "April, of course. Tomorrow is Good Friday."

"APRIL! It can't be!" Three nights. That was all. *If you say so*, Merlin had said.

"Well, it is. Trevor hasn't heard from you since the beginning of January. He's been scared witless. He thought you might have . . . done something stupid."

Cal knew what that meant. Struggling to keep calm, he said, "What did you tell him?"

"That I'd seen you here, in Bath, that you were okay. I told him you'd be ringing him tonight. You're going to do it, too."

He was stunned into silence. "It was only a few days."

She smiled, too brightly. "Maybe you lost track of time."

He didn't want to think about it. "We've changed places," he said gravely.

She laughed. "Sort of."

"I suppose your parents will have a fit when they come home. Like Trevor did when you came." He smiled sadly. "Though you were better off than him all along."

"My parents won't be home." She stood up and went to the door, so that he couldn't see her face. "Mummy's in London, as usual. Dad's abroad." She opened the hall door and yelled, "Anytime, Marj," and then came back.

Cal looked up at her. "Anytime what?"

"Food."

It came on a trolley, and they ate it at the big table in the window, looking out onto a green lawn and flowerbeds of wallflowers and bluebells. In the spring twilight a flock of blue tits pecked and fought over a full bird table.

The meal was Italian, soup and then pasta, and he was glad it wasn't spaghetti because he couldn't eat that properly, and then some sweet like a trifle he'd never had before. Shadow had wine and he had orange juice. He ate quickly, trying not to. The stiff white cloth and heavy knives and forks, the starched napkins and the table settings made it seem like a restaurant, with Marj as the waitress. He thought of Hawk's microwave. "Have you seen Hawk?"

Shadow sighed. She licked her spoon. "I'd better tell you what happened. After Trevor took you off that night, we went back to the farmhouse and the police were there. My parents were with them. My mother threw her arms round me; she wept and sobbed. My father looked embarrassed. Arthur was grave. Kai laughed. I knew I'd have to go with her. She would have made trouble for them all, for Hawk especially. If she even found out I'd been traveling with him . . . So I came back. It was blackmail, pure and simple. Though I told Hawk I'd be back in the summer holidays. I won't lose the Company, Cal. They mean too much."

He looked down. "How can you be unhappy here, Shadow? If I lived in a house like this, I could never be unhappy. Bath, your parents, it's . . . it's a world away . . ."

He stopped, as always. But she said, "You don't have to clam up anymore. I know all about your mother, Cal. Trevor told me. He and Thérèse came here, like I said." She put the spoon down angrily. "Why didn't you tell me they weren't your parents? Why didn't you tell me?" But she knew why.

He left the table and went over to the window. So she said to his back, "My mother's not like yours, no. A world away. She's rich, she's ambitious, she's on TV, a media queen. My father's in computing. He has his own firm. They live for their work. I never see them. I had a different au pair every year till I was twelve. Really privileged!" She got up and came behind him. "I live by myself, in all this splendor. I could have a car if I wanted. I could party and stay in the London flat and get high on drugs and they wouldn't know. I have an allowance for all the designer clothes I want. I have a trust fund and a gold credit card. They think this setup makes us a family but we're not. Her PA sends me my birthday present, can you believe that?"

Cal turned. "I'm sorry," he said. "I didn't understand."

"Not your fault. Your mother . . . she was a mess, she ruined things for you, but she was there. Mine never is. She wouldn't have been much bothered where I'd gone, except that some journalist got hold of the story and she thought it would spoil her precious career."

She was rigid, stepped away from him, turned her back. Suddenly he felt he had never known her, that the shadow was back between them.

"You've always thought, haven't you, that if you'd had money, it would have been different."

He nodded, bleak.

"Well, it isn't. Your life was worse than mine, I know that. But misery is misery, Cal. Loneliness is loneliness. And there's one thing about your mother that I'd bet on, one thing I've never had."

"What?" he whispered.

Shadow turned. Her eyes were wet; she smiled at him wanly. "I'll bet she loved you."

* Twenty-three *

Am I on the right road for the house of the Fisher King?
2nd Continuation

There were crystals hanging in the window. They swung softly in the drafts, and Cal watched the tiny brilliant rainbows they made on the walls, all moving together. He lay on the soft pillows, wonderfully comfortable.

Shadow's spare room was twice the size of his old room in the flat, larger even than the bedroom at Trevor's. The furniture was old and graceful, and the windows immensely tall, with white painted shutters that could close the night out. Now, late in the morning, he watched the sun, and thought of the Waste Land.

He had been wandering there three months. At least, out here it had been that long. For him, he didn't know how long it had been. He could only remember fragments, the burning tree, the chapel. You couldn't forget a whole quarter of a year. Unless your mind was breaking up.

In the comfort after his deep sleep he was oddly unworried. And that wasn't like him. Maybe he should see a doctor. He examined the idea idly, mulled it over, saw himself in waiting rooms, and then explaining, trying to explain, to a man behind a large wooden desk. "It's as if time went differently there. But Merlin said . . ."

The doctor would lean forward, interested. "Merlin?" he would say.

"Yes. One of Arthur's men."

The doctor would make notes rapidly.

Despite himself, Cal grinned and stretched. If he was going crazy, at least this morning he didn't care. Until he thought of his mother.

He got up instantly, dressed in his borrowed clothes, and went downstairs, looking through the tall, sunny rooms of the house. Finally he found Shadow sitting out in a sort of conservatory, reading, a fat white cat on her lap. She looked up. "God, you can sleep!"

"I was tired."

She was wearing the other clothes this morning, the ones she'd worn in Chepstow, the filmy black, the boots. It made her look more familiar, despite her clean face. She pushed the cat off. "Let's go out for something to eat."

It was holiday time and Bath was busy. Down in the town

they found a small café full of American tourists and squeezed into a table at the back. Shadow ordered pizza and chips and Cokes and Cal said bleakly, "I haven't got any money."

She put a credit card on the table. "Daddy can pay."

"Shadow . . ."

"Forget it. What did Trevor have to say?"

Cal sighed. The conversation had not been pleasant. "He was furious. Where had I been? Didn't I know Thérèse was worried stiff? Didn't I know the police in three counties were out looking for me?"

She nodded. "Sounds familiar. And when he'd calmed down?"

Cal drank the Coke. "Said the job was still there if I wanted it."

"Do you?"

He gazed out at the packed streets. Then he said, "I used to dream, at home. All I ever wanted was somewhere clean, quiet. Everywhere I went I'd look at the big houses and be sick with envy of the kids who came out of them. I still am. I can't just turn that off. And that takes money."

Shadow waited till the waitress had put the plates down and gone. Then she said, "So that's a no, then."

He looked up at her, a sudden grin. "I suppose it is."

"Sophie?"

She looked up, alert. Then said, "Hi, Marcus. Cal, this is Marcus. I told you about him."

He was big, blond, expensive. Public school, by the voice. His sunglasses would have cost a few days' salary. Cal stood up, found he was taller and enjoyed that. "Hi," he said quietly.

Marcus looked at him, then at Shadow. "Thought we might go out somewhere tonight, if you're interested. But. . ." he shrugged, "no bother."

She smiled sweetly. "Maybe another time."

"Fine." He went, looking back once. Cal sat back down and glanced at Shadow. She laughed softly. "Perfect," she said.

Afterward they went shopping, Shadow buying a strange hand-painted T-shirt for herself, and a sweater for him, even though he told her not to. Such casual spending appalled and thrilled him. It was like another world.

In the Body Shop he lounged while she picked over various shampoos, leaning against the green-painted counter idly. Then his gaze froze.

Leo was looking in through the window. The big man was watching Cal; as soon as he saw Cal notice him he turned and was gone in the flood of pedestrians. Cal yelled, "Shadow!" and raced out.

People buffeted him. He pushed through them, turned right up Milsom Street and ran, jumping impatiently out into the road where cars hooted. Up ahead Leo's huge back was clear. He crossed into an alley. Just behind, Cal sprinted between vans, dodged a stroller, threw himself around the corner. "Hey! WAIT!"

The man turned. He was a total stranger.

Cal's breath almost choked him.

Behind him, Shadow turned the corner, breathing hard. "Cal! Who was it?"

He looked around at the totally ordinary town, then at her face, the hidden concern. He rubbed his hair with a shaky hand. "I think it's me, isn't it?" he whispered.

You had to pay for deckchairs in the park. It was like you had to pay for everything in the world. Devastated, he sat there and knew he had imagined it all. Unless he could find Corbenic again. Unless he could find the Grail.

They both sat silent in the sun until she said, "Look, Cal . . ."

He sat up, interrupting. "I'm going to Glastonbury. Will you come with me?"

"Why there?"

"Merlin said in all the stories the Grail is there."

"Merlin's mad. I mean," she said hastily, "he may be right about that, but this place you found . . . this hotel, was up north. Right?"

Suspicious, he looked at her. The truth came to him, blinding and brilliant as the flashing rainbows in the bedroom. "You don't believe any of it. The bleeding spear, the Grail . . ."

"I think you stayed the night at some hotel. That you saw

some . . . people carrying things. It must have been a bit odd."

"A bit odd!" Aghast, he stood up and stared down at her. "I thought you at least would understand."

Shadow bit a nail. "It's like Hawk. He thought he was someone from the past. They all had this game, that they were immortals. I never knew if they were winding me up. Then I thought, they believe this. So I believed it. If you believe something hard enough, it comes true. In a way. What he said to you about the Grail is just another old story."

He came and sat down. "You think I'm going the way my mother did."

"I think you're looking for something that's not here. Maybe you're looking for her. You won't find her in Glastonbury." It was cruel, he thought bitterly, and maybe Shadow thought so too, because she said quietly, "I never knew her, remember."

Out of his anger he shrugged. "I often thought I'd like to tell you. Have someone to moan about it to."

"Tell me now," she said gently.

He didn't know where to start. There was too much. The dirt, the drink, the time she'd come at him with the broken bottle. So he said, "Once, she cut herself."

"What?"

"I'd come home late, and she'd cut herself. With the kitchen knife. Long, red slashes, on her arms. Blood everywhere, on her sleeves, the sofa, everywhere."

Shadow was rigid. "What did you do?"

"Freaked out. Panicked. Mopped up. Got her to Casualty—God, we lived in that place. Locked up the knives. Lived with it, the terror of it happening again, rocked myself to sleep. Never told anyone." He looked up, stricken. "There's all that in me, Shadow, and I can't get it out. And I swore to her I'd be back for Christmas, I swore I would and I didn't go, and I knew, I knew what she might do! Don't you see, I can't live with that! I can't!"

He was shaking. His voice was broken up. "I've coped, always coped. Made rules. Never admitted . . . But now I'm lost, Shadow. I'm in pieces. There's nothing left." He was sobbing at last.

Shadow put her arms around him and held him tight and they sat together in the sunlight for a long time till he was calm, kids on skateboards going up and down the path in front of them, wheeling, their voices high in the bright air. Finally, confused, he rubbed his face and pulled away and said, "You didn't answer my question about Glastonbury."

"I can't come, Cal. I have to stay here now, and that's your fault. I promised I'd finish my exams and I will. I don't think you should go either, not on your own."

"I'm not . . ."

She turned to him. "Look. Stay a few days. Think about it. You'll feel better." She sounded choked. Then she lay back in the striped deckchair and closed her eyes against the ripple from the river. "There are two sorts of life, aren't there? The one that seems ordinary, like this, and then the reflection from it. Curved, shiny. All mixed up."

He should have known. Leaning over the mahogany banister that night he heard her voice, low and urgent. "He's not right. He's been sleeping rough for three months and can't remember any of it. And now this nonsense about Glaston-bury. Yes, but he needs to be home!"

Maybe Hawk said something; she laughed, low, but she wasn't amused. Then she said, "Tomorrow. First thing. I don't know what to do, Hawk. Just get here."

Back upstairs, he waited, watching his own gaunt face in the mirror. When she had gone to bed he sat there still, hear-ing the clock chime in the hall below, the slow cars in the street, the laughter of late-night drinkers. When he finally moved he was stiff; but he picked up the rucksack and went downstairs silently, and let himself out and walked down the long broad street without looking back.

Next morning, on the bus crossing the high plateau of Mendip, he thought of Merlin, because this was not how quests were achieved, not how the soul was saved, not squashed beside a fat woman with shopping bags and behind a kid defiantly smoking under a NO SMOKING sign. But he knew that unless he found Corbenic he would be lost, he could not move on. He would spend his life in regrets. He had caused his mother's death, he had lied to the Company and betrayed Shadow back into the life she detested, and there was nothing he could do about any of that. But Bron was left. He might still be able to tell Bron he'd been wrong. And if Bron was real then he was not going mad.

In Corbenic, there might be another chance.

She would be waking about now. On the end of her bed she would find the CD, and would be staring at it. *Listen to this*, he had scrawled on the cover.

Outside, now Bristol was left behind, the countryside was wide and green, the buds on the trees bursting with fresh leaf, the sky blue and windy with high cloud. They travelled through villages he had never heard of, with names out of lost stories: Farrington Gurney, Temple Cloud, Chewton Mendip, and people got off and on and the crush eased and the smoker was gone and he could breathe.

And then the bus came down through a steep wood of birch and turned a corner, and before him he saw a wide plain, flat as a chessboard with its tiny fields, and rising out of it like a conical, mystical hill from a medieval painting, was the Tor, crowned with its ruined church.

At the town's entrance the sign said THE ANCIENT AVALON. He hoped it still was. Though as he got off and a sudden shower turned the world gray, it seemed farther away from Corbenic than any other place that he'd been.

❉ Cup ❉

❀ Twenty-four ❀

Fair son, this castle is yours.
High History of the Holy Grail

He bought some food and spent a few hours sleeping in the corner of a grassy graveyard outside the church in the main street. Although he'd had some rest at Shadow's his whole body still seemed weary, as if the time in the Waste Land, the time that had not existed, was catching him up. And he was thin. Worn thin.

The first thing he did when he woke was to lie for a while watching the sky; the blueness of it slowly filling with great dark-edged clouds.

Then he sat up and pulled on the rucksack and walked down to the post office. He put the change from the fifty-pound note Shadow had given him in an envelope and posted it back to her. On the inside of the flap he scrawled, *I can't take any more.*

❀ Cup ❀

Glastonbury was a crazy place. All the shops had books about the Grail; he flicked through them and found they were full of theories, history, photographs. Everything was brightly colored, hanging with crystals, swords, pentangles, healing herbs. The noise and the people seemed to hurt his senses; he felt bruised, wanted somewhere quiet, anywhere green. Sometimes he struggled to breathe. Like a fish out of water.

At the cross in the center of town, he stopped and looked back up the pavement. A man in a bright stripy T-shirt was gazing intently into a shop window, face turned away. Thoughtful, Cal walked on.

Owein. One of the Company. They must have been watching this place the whole time. He scowled, furious with himself. He should have known that!

Quickly, he ducked around the corner and began to run, up the steep, shop-lined street toward the Tor. From the Tor you could see for miles. From the Tor you might see anything. He didn't look back till the last turning. There was no sign of anyone following. But Cal knew the Company; they were on to him now. They'd find him. They were his friends; they'd want to look after him. Get him home. But he could only find the castle on his own.

The footpath led over green hilly fields where yellow flies buzzed over dried cowpats and the hedges were white with cow parsley and campion. This was Chalice Hill, and beyond it, rising crazily, ridged in furrows and mysterious terraces, was the Tor. Crossing the last field toward it he saw the small moving specks that were people up there, and stopped, instantly still. *You could see for miles.* His own thought mocked him. So they'd have someone up there, wouldn't they, watching for him. He swore.

He waited till dark, holed up under a hedge. Slowly the daylight died, night coming early in a rush of high wind; it rustled the trees above him and the noise of cars and people faded until the wind became the only sound in the world, louder than he had thought it could ever be. When he sat up and brushed the leaves and soil off, it roared around him, buffeting him into the hedge, small raindrops spattering his face.

He crossed the small lane and began to climb. There was a concrete path, and then steps. They wound around the ridges of the strange hill; high steps, and soon he was breathless, but the higher he went the stronger the wind was, flapping the collar of his jacket and whipping his hair into his eyes, making him stagger as the steps came around to the west. Below, the countryside spread out, dark and shadowy on the flat levels, the roads marked with red streetlights, the whiter sprawl of house windows glinting, and beyond that the low hills, the far, far distant darkness of the sea, and Wales.

Cal stopped, his side aching. Then, carefully, he left the steps and scrabbled up the last steep slope, gripping for handholds in the slippery grass, digging his toes in and hauling himself up. Wind roared in his ears. He lay with his face close to the sweet-smelling turf, and peered over the top.

There was a tower—the tower of the old church. It rose, huge and black against the night sky. Inside it, small red glimmers, the reflections of a fire, danced and leaped.

He listened. There were voices, low voices talking. The flattened roar of the flames in a gust of wind. Crackles.

Carefully he pulled himself up and crouched, keeping low, off the skyline. Then he crawled to the long dark shadow of the tower and slid into it, into the corner made by the great buttress.

A tiny scatter of music came out. An advertisement for a concert in Bristol.

Cal grinned. He peered around the buttress and through the open archway, his hands gripping the crumbling, cold stones.

Two men were wrapped in blankets by the fire. Both were asleep. Beside them a radio bleated into a pop song, so thin that he knew its batteries were almost gone. As far as he could tell in the shadows, the men were strangers to him. But that didn't mean they weren't in the Company.

He stepped back, and back, watching them, but as they didn't move except to breathe he let the darkness cover him and turned, facing out, into the wind. It hurtled itself against him like some beast; he held his arms out to it, wide, letting the rain hit him so hard he felt it would bruise him. All across the miles of the wide Somerset levels it roared, and he was the first thing it met, high in its wild, raging storm path, and above him the osprey soared, wings wide, and below the land was dark, the lights going out one by one as he put them out deliberately in his mind, like the candles in Bron's banquet room.

And he saw Corbenic.

How could he have missed it?

It was huge, its windows blazed with light! No more than a mile away, it rose up out of the dark lands like a mass of granite, its walls and turrets outlined with torches, a vast castle, the only castle, a haphazard conglomerate of every castle he had ever seen, in every picture, film, book. It was a stronghold, invulnerable. Birds cawed and swirled over its highest pinnacles, sentinels patrolled its battlements. In its hundred courtyards horses were stabled. Blindfold hawks slept in its mews, cooks worked in its kitchens, a thousand servants, squires and serving maids, knights and women, poets and singers thronged its halls. This was how a castle should be.

And then the wind stung his eyes and it blurred and faded.

"Wait!" he shouted in panic. "Wait for me!"

"Cal." Her voice was close behind him. He turned and she was there, in the old sweater and trousers that never seemed clean.

He stepped back.

"I'm sorry," she whispered.

"You always said that."

"Did you think I never meant it?"

"I don't know." He shook his head, baffled. "I don't know, do I! If you meant it, why did you go on drinking? Why didn't you change? Why did you let the time go on, days, years, all that time. All the time that belonged to me! That should have been mine!" He was yelling, he knew. The wind took the words away as soon as he'd shouted them; it flung them out into the dark land.

His mother sat down on the grass, catching her hair to keep it from blowing across her eyes. "Because of the castle," she said wonderingly, looking out at it. "That was the reason." She smiled at him, and he saw she was calm, as she'd never been. "You see, Cal, I always thought they were voices but they weren't. They were echoes. No one explained that to me. I was hearing them and they were real, but not in the way I thought. And I hated hearing them, so I did anything to get away, to drown them. And I'm sorry, Cal, love, because it was always you that got hurt. The fear was so stifling I couldn't see through it. I couldn't. The voices were all the world, but that should have been you, my little boy, my son. All the things you missed out on, never did, never had. I can never give you that back, Cal."

It was as if she was speaking about someone else. As if all that was over. Long finished.

"I should have come home," he said bitterly.

She stood and reached out, her hand almost touching him. "When you left, all I thought of was your father. How he left. He never came back either."

Cal closed his eyes; only a stinging second of darkness. When he opened them she wasn't there, had never been there. The sudden emptiness of it was a torment, and he turned and looked out at the great castle, and suddenly tore the straps of the rucksack open and rummaged in it furiously, pulling out the crumpled card he had brought from the flat, with its childish rounded writing and the picture of the flowers, carefully drawn in crayon.

"Don't go without this!" he screamed. He opened his hand, and the wind took it. In a flap of sound it was there and it was gone.

The castle went with it.

And when the urgent voice behind him said, "Stand still, Cal. You're too near the edge," he even smiled as he turned.

Kai stood in his dark coat beside the tower. Behind him, in a wide semicircle, were some of the Company—Gwrhyr, Owein, a dozen of the Sons of Caw. And Hawk.

❀ Twenty-five ❀

I am a messenger to thee from Arthur, to beg thee come and see him.

Peredur

Cal stepped back. Behind him the sheer slope of the hill plummeted into darkness.

Kai looked anxious. "We're here to help."

"Then leave me alone." He glanced around at them. They were tense. They were afraid of what he might do. He realized how wild he must look and laughed, a hollow, vicious laugh that even scared him.

"For God's sake, Cal," Hawk said hoarsely. "We're your friends. We just . . ."

"How did you know where to find me? Shadow?"

Kai flashed a glance at Hawk; the big man nodded. "You can't blame her. She was worried."

Cal shook his head, savoring the irony. So she had done it

to him now. Stepped in, interfered. She had shown him what it felt like.

"Come back with us," Kai said quietly. "You can stay at Caerleon. No questions, no bother. The Company will look after you."

They only wanted to help; he knew that. So he said, "I can't. I have to find this place. Corbenic. I'm close to it, I know I am." He waved into the dark. "It's out there. Just out there."

Kai took a step to the side. "You say you've seen the Grail."

"And I don't suppose you believe me."

The tall man laughed calmly. "On the contrary, Cal. We know about the Grail. The search for it goes on always. Don't you think we haven't searched for centuries? But then, you don't believe us either, do you?"

For a long moment only the wind raged between them. Until Cal said, very quietly, "I believe you are who you think you are." Then he turned, and stepped off the edge.

Hawk's howl, the grab of his great hands, the thump of the grass: he remembered those, and then his whole body was out of control, a breathless, crashing, flailing roll down the sheer slope, banging, bruised, tumbled, flung out and smashed back against the ridges of the hill until he hit the stone and the night went black.

Maybe only for a second. Because when he came to, the pain was so intense he could hardly draw a breath, and he knew he'd broken a rib, maybe more than one. His arms and shoulders were so sore he groaned as he pushed himself up, but he could stand, and even run, in a doubled-up, uneven agony. The hill above him was alive with shouts and torches; they were coming down, skidding, wild with anxiety. He backed into a hedge, forced his way through, snapping the thick stalks of hemlock, wading through stiff grass.

"Cal!" Hawk's shout was a nightmare of fear; gasping, Cal stumbled away from it, through a field into the garden of a cottage, deep in weeds. They must think he'd broken his neck. It was a miracle he hadn't.

The castle had been close. Beyond Chalice Hill. At the bottom of the town.

There were hens in the garden; they cackled and set up a terrible clucking racket. Then a dog barked, and a back door opened.

Cal swore, flung himself at the wall and clambered over it. It hurt so much he had to stop then, coughing and retching, holding onto the wall to keep on his feet. Breathing was an agony. Maybe he should give up. Let them take him home.

Home. There was no home. Not Sutton Street, not Otter's Brook. Not the farm at Caerleon. Not Shadow's Georgian palace. None of them was his. Only Corbenic was his.

He lifted his head, dragged a breath in. "Show me," he hissed to the dark. "If you want me to come, show me."

"Cal!" They'd heard the hens. The yell was close. He ran,

loping down the lane, around the corner into the main road.

Amber lamplight dyed the night; cars droned past him, a truck. He ran along the narrow pavements, past the entrance to the Chalice Well, every breath a struggle, an ache clutched tight to his chest.

They were close; too close. He could never outrun them. He ducked off the road into a garage forecourt; it was closed and dark, but he slipped into the shadows and found a door-way and slid down onto his heels, head on knees, a knot of pain, gasping.

Footsteps. Running, then slow. Still.

Then Kai's voice. "He can't be far. He's in no state . . ."

"When we find him, let me talk to him." That was Hawk, sounding anguished.

"You two that way. The rest, up into the town. Work your way down to the abbey. Get a grip, Hawk of May. We'll find him."

Cal knew that was true. Kai was relentless, and would find him. Soon. He waited until it was quiet. Then edged out.

Glastonbury was silent. The pubs had shut and in the houses televisions flickered blue and gray behind the curtains. He walked slowly, warily, his footsteps echoing, his shadow lengthening as he left the lampposts behind, until he came to a high wall on the right and he knew this was the abbey, the grounds of which took up most of the center of town. But the castle had been here.

If he stayed on the road the Company would find him, so he reached up with both hands and grasped the top of the stonework, then dug his toes in and pulled. The pain was so staggering he let go at once and crumpled onto the pavement; he wanted only to lie there and die, but it was already too late.

A sound in the street made him turn. Two dark figures flitted behind a parked car.

Instantly, without letting himself think about it, he grabbed the wall and climbed, got to the top, kicked out at the sudden tight grip on his ankle. Then he was over and running across the dark expanse of lawn, racing toward the twin stark ruins of the abbey, and behind him boots were scrambling over the wall, Hawk was calling his name, and his heart was thudding behind the pain of his ribs as if it would burst out.

"Where?" he gasped. "Where?"

The building was a bewilderment of shadows; in the cold dimness of the windy night its trees roared and small fragments of masonry rattled from the snapped stumps of windows. Cal swung into the vast roofless nave and stopped dead.

A man was sitting on an enclosed rectangle of grass there. A big man, in a scruffy tweed jacket. He stood up slowly. He seemed unsurprised.

Cal held out his hands. "Don't try to stop me."

Arthur nodded. He looked down at the stone. "This is my grave," he said wryly.

"What?"

"Only that nothing is what it seems. Death, even. It's never too late, Cal."

Shadow was with him. She was sitting so still Cal barely registered her; the tattoo was back on her face, and for a second then he was absolutely certain that none of this was real, that it was all in his mind and that he'd wake soon, in the room at Trevor's maybe, and hear Thérèse singing in the bathroom.

Shadow stood up, and said, "What will happen if you find it?"

"Bron will be healed. I'll be healed. There will be no Waste Land."

Sadly, she shook her head. "Will you come back?"

"Would you want me to?"

"Of course." She glared at him.

"Then I'll come back. If I can."

She went to step toward him, but Arthur held her wrist. "That's all I want," she whispered. And for a second, it was all he wanted. Then he sidestepped past her, and saw the castle. It was there, over the grass. Heedless, he ran toward its open gates.

"Cal! Be careful!" The shout was Hawk's, close; Cal turned, stumbled backward, tripped over some stonework.

Then he fell with a splash and a yell, and before he could even breathe, water closed over his face. He kicked, fought, swallowed black gunge, found the air, coughed it up, sank. Darkness filled his eyes and nostrils, choked his throat, rose into his lungs, webbed his mouth, trapping an unheard scream like a bubble that grew and grew and would never burst, and he was caught and tangled in a net of terror, drowning, dying, dead, surely, till the big hands came down and hauled him out, into an explosion of air, a lifting, a gripping of the wet grass with both hands, a retching, vomiting relief.

The hands held him tight, around his shoulders, till he had finished. Then they peeled the wet strands of net from his hair, passed him a rag that he took and wiped his face with, his fingers trembling with exhaustion. Finally, shaking, sick, desperate, he looked up.

"So," Leo said sourly. "It's you."

❊ Twenty-six ❊

What we have been longing for ever since we were ensnared by sorrow is approaching us.

Parzival

He was on the banks of a lake; above him a steep slope rose, spindly birch trees rustling against the dim sky. The wind was loud here too, rushing in the branches. There was no abbey, no pursuit. Instead only the black waters rippled, sloshing against the reed bed.

"I came out of that?" he whispered.

Leo laughed mirthlessly. "Didn't we all?" He pulled on a rope; Cal saw the small wooden boat loom out of the night.

"Get in," the big man said.

Weary, Cal clambered in and sat, bent over the pain in his chest. He was soaked and cold and couldn't stop shivering. There was nothing to wrap around himself but his arms, so he gritted his teeth and stammered, "I've seen you. And the girl."

"Can't have," Leo muttered.

"It's true. A few times. And the osprey."

"Not us." The oars dipped rhythmically; the boat rocked on the current. Leo was a silhouette of blackness. "We don't leave here."

"I know what I saw!"

"Do you?" The voice was acid. "You weren't so sure of it last time you were here. You didn't see a thing then."

Furious, Cal shut up. When he could speak again it was in a quieter voice. "I was wrong."

Leo rowed, saying nothing.

The wind buffeted them, and when the stone quay appeared out of the darkness Leo had to struggle to lay the boat against it; he grabbed Cal and handed him out roughly, so that Cal stumbled and turned angrily. But there was no one in the boat.

For a moment Cal stood staring at it; then he turned away. Because this was Corbenic. This was not a place where anything was as it seemed.

There was a small thread of path upward; he followed it, gasping and grabbing at tree trunks and low branches to haul himself up. The pack on his back weighed him down; he tugged it off, and threw it into the bushes. But before he had taken two steps he went back, and pulled out the broken pieces of the sword.

At the top was the lane. It looked just the same: dark, wet, leading into nowhere between high hedges. But now the sky had a streak of brightness, and there was a blackbird singing somewhere, as if the dawn was coming.

He turned right, and came almost at once to a vast gatehouse. It must be the front entrance; it was not the way he'd come before. Torches of wood dipped in pitch smoked acridly in brackets on the wall; the gate was wide open but overgrown with ivy, as if it had been years since it was closed. Cal walked beneath it, and stopped in its shadow.

Before him was a wide, paved courtyard; on each side the gray walls of the castle rose into darkness. The courtyard was empty. Great weeds sprouted between its cracked stones; the half doors of the stables hung askew. There was no sound. Only the wind whistled in the high stonework and the windows; the castle was derelict, a stillness of shadows, its blown dust eddying in tiny whirlpools in the lee of buttresses. He had found Corbenic, and it was deserted.

He gripped the sword tight. "Bron!" His voice was small, pitiful; he scowled and called again. "BRON. I'VE COME BACK!"

No one answered.

A bat, high in the sky, flitted briefly between turrets. The wind gusted a shutter, banging it so that Cal turned instantly. Only the blank windows looked down at him.

He was too late. Maybe the mistakes he had made—no, not mistakes, the lie he had told, his betrayal—had been too much.

Maybe he would search the world and beyond it for all of his life and he would never see the Grail again. Maybe you only had one chance, and he had blown it, as he had with his mother.

He went on, quickly now, over the slabbed yard, in through a rusted portcullis, squeezing through a gap, forcing the brittle bars to snap.

It was not the same. It was worse. The stairs were there, and the wide banqueting hall, but it had no roof now and the trees had sprouted inside; the ivy was a mass of leaves and the only table left was rotten and soft with green lichen and pulpy mushroomy growths, yellow in the paling light. Paneling had fallen from the walls; a chandelier lay in pieces among the brambles and willow herb; as he pushed his way through, glass cracked and crushed under his feet.

He found a door and beyond it was a corridor, filthy with dust, blocked halfway down by a roof-fall. Desperate, he forced his way back and found the stairs, but they were a tangle of bindweed and as he climbed them they became soft, creaking ominously, so that by the turn in the elegant ruined balustrade he dared not go farther.

"Bron!" he called, his voice hoarse. "Please. For God's sake!"

They were dead. All dead. Because they had never been here. He was as ill as his mother had been, undiagnosed.

He turned, sat down. His whole strength seemed to go. His legs were weak; he couldn't stand, or breathe. As he doubled up he felt the whole staircase creak, an infinitesimal shift. It was unsafe, on the verge of collapse. But he didn't care. He threw the sword down, at his feet.

Upstairs, a door creaked. He jerked around. It was above him, up there in the hanging rooms, the floorless corridors. As if someone was there.

He stood. "Where are you?" he whispered.

A whisper of sound. The drag of material over dust, a soft slither.

He grabbed the hilted end of the sword, held it tight.

And then, a flame. Tiny, in the distance, a candle flame; flickering, barely there, but it was coming toward him down the long corridor, as if it was being carried, carefully, with a hand cupped around it to keep off the drafts. In its light he saw doorways, a gilt mirror, a sweep of cobweb.

And a woman. The edge of her face. Her hair. On the broken landing she paused and looked down at him. "Come home, Cal," she whispered. Her voice was far.

He took two more fast steps up, then the stairway was broken off, the shattered remains lying far below. "I can't . . ." he breathed.

She held out her hand. "Please."

The flame flickered red over her hair; lit the blond highlights. They looked right.

For a moment he paused. Then he tossed the sword pieces over; they landed with ringing cracks that echoed through the vast ruin like lightning. He closed his eyes. And he walked on up the staircase.

There were no steps, and he knew that, and he knew that if he looked down he was lost, but he could make them come, he could feel them under his feet and they were solid, and when he felt her hand grab him she was solid too, and even before he opened his eyes he knew that he had forgiven her, that he had loosed hold of that anger, that he had made the world be as he wanted it to be, because the world was inside him.

She was laughing, proud, and outside the wind was roaring, and she hugged him tight. "You did that for me!" she said. He hugged her too, and then he kissed her, as he had not done for years. When she pulled away he saw she had the sword pieces in her hands, and that the candle was burning in its holder on the floor, though now there were two of them, tall slim tapers.

He nodded. He couldn't speak, but he held out his hand and took the sword handle from her, very gently. She held the blade.

Together they fitted the pieces together. The metal joined. It locked. Its very atoms rearranged. It was whole, and Cal held it steady, and she put her hands over his; they were cool and strong and together they held the weapon tight.

"I love you, Cal," she said to him. "I always loved you. Before you were born I loved you. When you left, when you didn't come. Drunk. Sober. Always."

He looked away, then back at her. His breath came, shuddering. The sword was in his hand and the words came from him like small red moments of joy and terror, and as he said them they burned his lips, because they were true. "I love you too," he said. "I love you too."

He was alone. He was in the banqueting hall. The roof was new, the floor swept, a great fire roared in the hearth. Around the room the candles were lighting themselves, sparking on, great banks and stands and sconces full of them, a brilliance of wax.

People appeared, out of the air, out of nowhere, halfway through a sentence, talking, drinking, winking into existence without even noticing; a juggler catching balls he'd never thrown up, a steward pouring wine into a cup that was there just in time to receive it. Music sounded, midtune, harps, viols, a gallery of harmony. Servants walked out of emptiness carrying trays that filled, second by second, with grapes and fruit and cheeses; a spit appeared over the fire and then a boar to roast on it, hot fat spatting and dripping into the flames. Heat came, and laughter, and smells of mint and rosemary and cabbage and crusty bread. Chatter came, a thousand voices. Clatter, birdsong, the osprey's squawk.

And all the while, across the room, Bron was watching him. The Fisher King's eyes were dark. He sat still, and watched Cal, until Cal had to come toward him, sidestepping the juggler, the dancers. When he stood on the other side of the great table, food appearing between them, its smells and steams, Bron said, "I feared you would never come back."

"So did I," Cal said quietly.

"You're hurt."

"That makes two of us."

Bron smiled wryly. He looked over Cal's shoulder. "You've done well."

Leo came out of the crowd almost smiling. The big man's fingers tightened on the handles of the chair.

"I've been a fool," Cal said to them both.

"And now you have made your world again." Bron nodded, his face gaunt. "Look. It comes."

The crowds were quieting. They moved apart.

"I don't know what to do or say," Cal said rapidly. He turned back, panicky. "I don't understand what's happening, what I'm supposed to be."

Bron nodded. "I know."

"Then tell me!"

"I am the Grail's guardian. You will be too, one day. When the time is right."

"I want Shadow here, and Hawk and Kai. I want Merlin. And Thérèse!"

"They are here," Bron said tensely, "if you want them to be."

And they were, he saw, in the crowd, watching, silent, Shadow with her dark straight hair, and Merlin slouched at a table, the dog's head on his knees. They were here, in some way, because he was here and they were part of him, and that was enough. Even Trevor was there in an impeccable suit, and Phyllis from the office, drinking wine, and Arthur, leaning just inside the door, and quite suddenly he realized that amongst this crowd were all the people he had ever met in his life: Sally and Rhian, the train conductor, men and women he vaguely recognized or had no memory of, as if he'd maybe just passed them in the street once, and that was enough. Old teachers, schoolkids, enemies, doctors, all his mother's men, all her cronies from the pub.

He turned back. "What do I do?" he said, desperate. "What do I do?"

Bron's face was gaunt with tension. "You just look, Cal."

The doors were opening. Into the silence the light came, that glorious, golden light, the two boys with their candles, and behind them the tall, pale boy, the one with the lance. Bright red, the drops of blood fell from it; they made a trail across the floor, spattering on the shaven wood and the scattered trampled rushes, soaking in.

And behind them, the girl came, with the Grail. She held it high, and he saw that this time it was covered with a white cloth, but even then the light burned from it, the fierce white purity that he remembered, that he'd longed for, a light that scorched him and warmed him and gave him peace, and the people looked down, away, anywhere but at it. But the girl looked at Cal.

He recognized her. She was younger, his age. Before the nightmare, the drink, before everything had gone wrong with her. She was young and calm and strong, and she carried the vessel without fear, and she crossed the room and paused at the secret door with it.

Cal turned to Bron. *"Who drinks from the Grail?"* he whispered.

The room was utterly silent. Then Bron put both hands on the table, and gripped it, and with a terrible, almighty effort he pulled himself up shakily, and he and Cal were face to face. Leo kept close, but Bron was standing, shaking, exhausted, his knuckles white on the table edge. When he spoke his voice was hoarse with joy. "You do, Cal," he said.

Cal nodded, and turned. The Grail was carried through the secret doorway. He went after it, into a room brilliant with light. She handed him the cup, fingers over fingers, and he drank from it.

And he drank in its light, its terrors, its marvels. He saw the flame and the blood and the five mystical transformations, and when he handed it back to her he was healed, and she took it from him, and they laughed.

✤ Twenty-seven ✤

No one should repeat or describe the great wonders he encountered,
which gave him many fearful moments. Anyone who does so
will be sorry, for they are part of the mystery of the Grail.

1st Continuation

Shadow turned from the window and came to the edge of the bed. "When we pulled you out of the lake you weren't even breathing. Hawk and Kai worked on you for at least five minutes. We thought you were dead, Cal." She sat on the tie-dyed coverlet, and took his raw, scuffed fingers, trying to pin down the change in his face, understand the story he'd told her.

"Maybe I was," he said.

She smiled wryly. "What did you see when you drank? Visions? Dreams?"

"I can't tell you. Not that."

Outside a soft drizzle was bringing the cherry blossom down in drifts in the abbey grounds. Easter bells were ringing from the church in the High Street. The Company had lit a fire; its smoke drifted through the van.

"And the Waste Land. Is it healed?"

Cal lay back and looked at her. "I think it must be," he whispered.

And thus it is told of the Castle of Wonders.